Jason knows he must stay away from Mandy if he is to stay true to his father's dream.

He loved her more now than eight years ago. He loved the woman she'd become. He smiled into the darkness, thinking of her independent spirit, the cheerful manner in which she made her way through life without allowing problems and challenges and disappointments to trample her, the way Christ's love for others flowed so naturally from her.

He and Mandy shared a love for the mountains. He'd missed them horribly during the years spent in New York pursuing his father's dream for him. Eight years ago he'd asked Mandy to give up the mountains she loved for him. Now he knew he couldn't ask anyone he loved to give up something she loved that much—even if Mandy were willing. And what indication did he have that she was any more willing now than when he'd asked her to marry him?

He was jumping the proverbial gun, of course. Just because she returned his kisses tonight didn't mean she still loved him. Mandy wasn't the kind of woman who kissed a man unless she cared for him, but love—well, that might be a bit of a stretch.

One thing he knew for certain: There could be no more kisses. There was no place for their relationship to go if they moved past friendship. The more time they spent in each other's arms, the more painful the inevitable breakup.

He'd explain to her tomorrow. He hated the thought. It would be easier to just avoid her, but the easy way out was seldom the kindest.

He rolled over and buried his face in his pillow. He shut his mind to the memory of Mandy's kisses. The joy that filled him when he came to bed retreated, flooded out by the choice he'd made [illegible] dream instead of his own.

JOANN A. GROTE lives in Minnesota where she grew up. She uses the state for most of her story settings, and like her characters, JoAnn seeks to serve Christ in her work. She believes that readers of novels can receive a message of salvation and encouragement from well-crafted fiction. She has had several novels published with Barbour Publishing in the **Heartsong Presents** line as well as in the American Adventure series for kids.

Books by JoAnn A. Grote

HEARTSONG PRESENTS

HP36—The Sure Promise
HP51—The Unfolding Heart
HP55—Treasure of the Heart
HP103—Love's Shining Hope
HP120—An Honest Love
HP136—Rekindled Flame
HP184—Hope That Sings
HP288—Sweet Surrender
HP331—A Man for Libby
HP377—Come Home to My Heart
HP476—Hold on My Heart
HP496—Meet Me with a Promise

For a Father's Love

JoAnn A. Grote

Heartsong Presents

For my brother-in-law, Mark Falvey, because he's a wonderful father and because he keeps my computer running. And for my dear friend Patricia Thomas—thanks for your medical expertise. (Any mistakes related to medical situations in this story are mine.)

A note from the author:
I love to hear from my readers! You may correspond with me by writing:

JoAnn A. Grote
Author Relations
PO Box 719
Uhrichsville, OH 44683

ISBN 1-58660-631-X

FOR A FATHER'S LOVE

PRINTED IN THE U.S.A.

one

Jason punched the speakerphone button, irritated by the incessant buzz. His secretary wouldn't put through a call this afternoon unless it was important, but he still resented the intrusion. He faced a mountain of information to wade through before the corporate takeover meeting the next morning.

"J. P. Garth, here," he barked, scowling at the financial statement on his desk.

"Jason, it's—"

"Mandy." He dropped into the high-backed leather chair. His heart plunged to his stomach. The eight years since he'd heard her voice rolled away in a millisecond.

"I–it's your grandfather, Jason. He's had a heart attack."

"Heart attack? But he's strong as an ox." Jason's mind immediately built a foundation for his denial. Years of working on the mountainside Christmas tree farm kept Gramps in great shape. Besides, if he'd a heart attack, why would Mandy be the one to call? Last he knew, she lived more than an hour's drive from his grandparents.

He heard her take a shaky breath. "Your Grandma Tillie and I are at the hospital. She asked me to call you."

Fear surged through him. It must be true if Gram couldn't make the call herself. She was one tough lady. "Is he. . .is he dying?"

"No, but Dr. Monroe said it's an acute attack. They took an EKG and put Grandpa Seth on an IV with a drug to dissolve the clot in his heart. He started feeling better almost immediately."

"But he's still in danger?"

"Not after the clot dissolves. Not immediate danger. They'll have to do tests to see whether he needs angioplasty or bypass surgery."

"Bypass surgery?"

"Jason, I—"

"Tell Gramps and Gram I'll catch the next plane home."

He heard her sigh of relief. "Good. They need you."

Guilt pushed at his fear. He hadn't seen his grandparents since Christmas, ten months earlier. "Mandy. . ." Even with the arrangements to make and his fear for his grandfather, Jason hated to break the only connection he'd had with her since graduating from college.

"Yes?"

"Thanks."

"Good-bye, Jason."

He hung up, then took a deep breath and punched the button connecting him with his secretary. "Ida, get me on the next flight to Greensboro or Charlotte, North Carolina."

"What about the meeting tomorrow?"

"Neal will tell you what arrangements to make for it. First, get me on a flight."

"Yes, Sir."

Moments later Jason entered the senior partner's office through huge paneled doors and succinctly explained the situation to Neal.

After a few words of sympathy, Neal scowled. "Sounds like there's nothing you can do for him at the moment. Meetings on the Sullivan takeover begin tomorrow. We both know they're going to be rough. Can't you wait a few days?"

"No."

"He's your grandfather, J. P., not your father."

Jason leaned both hands on the senior partner's desk. "My parents died when I was a teenager. My grandparents took me in. They're as close to parents as it gets. I'm going home."

"I didn't realize," Neal blustered. "Of course, under the circumstances, a few days is understandable."

"I might be gone for more than a few days."

"What can you do for him if he's lying around recuperating?"

"He may be a grandfather, but his age doesn't keep him

from running his own Christmas tree farm."

"It's only the end of October. Surely he doesn't need you yet."

"Just starting the busiest time of year."

"But the takeover—"

"Timmins has been working with me on it. I know he's a junior partner and hasn't handled any negotiations alone, but he's a good man. He knows the facts in this case and my strategy. Every man jumps out on his own sometime. Guess this is Timmins's time."

Neal's face paled. "This is the largest case we've handled in three years. We can't entrust it to a tenderfoot."

"He can call me if he needs advice. You'll sit in on the meetings. Teamed with your prestige and experience, Timmins can pull it off. You hired him, Man. Put a little faith in him."

"I hired him for his potential. It takes more experience than he's had, even with your excellent tutoring, to pull off a coup like the one we plan." Neal tapped his fingertips on the mahogany desktop. "Let's postpone."

"If you postpone, our opponents will think we're waffling. You and Timmins can pull the meeting off. I need to catch a flight. I'll call you from North Carolina." Jason turned on his heel and left Neal protesting to empty space.

❧

It had been dark for hours when Jason's flight left New York. He leaned back in the wide, first-class seat, slowly removed his tie, and pulled his shoulders down, trying to stretch. Would his muscles never relax? He should sleep—he'd need his strength tomorrow—but his body wouldn't cooperate.

He glanced toward the window and saw his pale reflection there. His short brown hair looked crisply neat as always, the style chosen to present a dignified, self-confident business image, the same as his clothing. His eyes stared back at him from beneath almost straight, dark brows in a lean face. The ghostly image didn't show the lines that at thirty-two were already making inroads. All hints of the boy who grew up in

North Carolina's Blue Ridge Mountains had long since left his face. *And left my heart,* he thought, turning away from the window.

What would he find at his grandparents' mountain home? Would Gramps be better or worse? *Or might he?* . . .

Jason couldn't finish the thought.

A vision of his grandfather slid through Jason's mind: thick white hair, a trim white beard bordering a broad, tanned face with a permanent smile. His chest tightened. In many ways, Gramps had been more of a father to Jason than his own father. Sam Garth's position as professor of finance at the local university had supplied the family's material needs. He'd stressed to Jason the importance of responsibility and had groomed Jason for a successful career. But it was Gramps who had loved Jason unconditionally.

Jason lost his father when he was sixteen, half a lifetime ago. Now he might be losing Gramps. The tightness in his chest grew tauter.

He turned his thoughts deliberately from his fears. *Mandy.* Closing his eyes and leaning his head back against the seat, he let her voice drift through his memory. Had she been visiting Gram and Gramps at the time of the heart attack? She'd always liked them. He smiled, recalling how she called them Grandma Tillie and Grandpa Seth. He'd often suspected in the four years they dated that she loved his grandparents almost as much as she loved him.

As much as I thought she loved me.

Wouldn't he ever get over her refusal to marry and move to New York with him? He remembered everything about the day he'd proposed: the way the sunlight shone through the trees, adding copper lights to her brown hair, the determination in her wonderful, fir-green eyes, and the words that ripped his world apart: "I'll never leave the mountains, not for you, not for anyone."

He loved the mountains too, but when his parents died, he'd abandoned his dream of owning a tree farm like his grandfather's and embraced the career his father had wanted for him—a career in finance in New York City, the nation's financial hub.

Wasn't that what love did—sacrifice its own desires for the loved one? He'd trusted Mandy's love completely, but she hadn't loved him enough to sacrifice her precious mountains for a life with him.

"Mandy," he whispered. He rubbed a hand down his face. Turning his thoughts from his grandfather to Mandy had only replaced one kind of pain with another, more familiar one.

two

"Ooh, aren't you beautiful." Mandy Wells lifted the fragile angel from its protective wrappings. The morning sun streamed through the large window behind her, its rays resting on the tiny porcelain head, bringing to life the pink cheeks, blue eyes, and blond hair.

Mandy smoothed the angel's flowing gown of ivory satin and hand-spun lace, which was in striking contrast to her own faded blue jeans and oversized topaz sweater. "You'll be perfect for the top of the tree beside the door." Stepping quickly over cardboard packing boxes, Mandy made her way through the layer of crushed newspaper and Styrofoam beads covering the wooden floor.

She touched a switch, and the Christmas shop burst into life. Dozens of trees sparkled with every type of ornament. Spicy cinnamon and orange odors from Christmas potpourri and pine scent from swags hanging from wooden beams filled the air.

She stopped beside a tree decorated with Victorian nosegays, miniature dolls, wide ribbons of cream and pink, and sprays of baby's breath. Dragging a decorated wooden stool over, Mandy climbed up to remove a lace-backed nosegay of rose and cream buds from the treetop. Holding her breath, she stretched to attach the angel to the treetop.

Brass bells above the door jangled merrily. Mandy gasped as the door crashed into her stool.

"O-oh!" Mandy clutched the precious angel in one hand and grasped for the bedecked tree with the other. The tree tumbled to the floor. The stool slipped from beneath her. Mandy shut her eyes in anticipation of a hard landing.

There was a loud masculine grunt. Muscular arms closed

about her, crushing her against a hard chest with the delicate angel between her and her rescuer. The man lurched back with the sudden force of her weight. The door thudded shut when he crashed against it, the bells once again tinkling merrily.

She opened her eyes slowly. Finely cut light brown hair topped the ruggedly handsome face above her. The lips were colorless, the square jaw tensed, the green eyes wide with shock.

She knew those eyes. "Jason." The name came out in a hoarse whisper. Every nerve ending tingled to life. She thought she'd braced herself for the moment they'd meet. *Obviously I deluded myself.*

The shock in his eyes shifted to anger. Their fury brought Mandy back to her senses. She squirmed slightly. "If you'll let me go," she suggested, congratulating herself silently on her calm tone.

He set her roughly on her feet, steadying her with strong hands on her waist.

Instantly she regretted the lack of his arms about her. She'd longed to be back in those arms for years. *Idiot,* she reprimanded herself. She brushed the angel's golden hair into place, searching for time to compose herself. "You're certainly the man for the moment."

"Are you all right?"

He didn't look as though he cared. "I'm fine." She set the angel on the counter behind her, then turned to survey the scattered nosegays and broken miniature Victorian dolls. "Unfortunately, my tree didn't have as soft a landing."

Jason scowled at the rubble he'd created, then scanned the shop. "What is this place?"

She clasped her hands behind her back and surveyed the large room with its decorated Christmas trees, satin angels, and glittering snowflakes dangling from the wooden beams. Red-and-green stockings stuffed with toys hung from the oak mantel above the stone fireplace in the middle of the former barn, and brightly wrapped packages were piled everywhere.

"It's a Christmas store. I thought so, but since you didn't recognize it as such, I thought I'd better give it another look."

He took a deep breath. "What are you and this store doing in Gramps's barn?" The question came slowly, each word forced between clenched teeth.

She took a couple steps back and stared at him in surprise. "Your grandparents never told you? They leased it to me last January."

"Why?"

She couldn't pretend she didn't know what he meant by that one-word question. "The short answer is that last year when I bought my Christmas tree from them, I told them my dream of opening a Christmas store in a barn like this. They'd just built that long warehouse-type building for their tree business, so they offered me this barn. I accepted, and"—she spread her arms toward the store—"here I am with my Christmas store."

"You know what I meant."

You meant why would they let me use the barn only a few hundred yards from their house when they know how much you and I meant to each other once; why would I want to be so close to the only family you have left. "Can't a more complete explanation wait? You must be eager to see your grandfather. Or have you just come from the hospital?"

"No, I haven't seen him yet. I thought Gram would be at the house and we could go to the hospital together."

She noticed the circles beneath his eyes. She'd been avoiding his eyes, avoiding looking at that face she saw all too often in her dreams. Stubble shadowed his cheeks. His finely tailored gray suit was wrinkled; the white shirt with its monogrammed pocket was rumpled and open at the neck. The tip of a navy-and-gray-striped tie poked from a suit pocket. Obviously he hadn't slept all night.

The realization softened her tone. "I took Grandma Tillie in to the hospital this morning."

"Already? The sun's barely up."

"She couldn't sleep last night. She wants to be with your grandfather every minute."

"I guess that's no surprise. She and Gramps have spent almost sixty years together."

His green-eyed gaze gentled, holding her own. Her throat tightened, remembering they'd promised to love each other as long and as fully as Grandma Tillie and Grandpa Seth. Was Jason remembering too? She shifted her gaze to the floor to break the spell, but the taut feeling in her chest stayed.

Jason cleared his throat. "You say Gramps is doing okay?"

She glanced back at him, ashamed at daydreaming about the two of them when Grandpa Seth was so ill. "He's doing as well as can be expected."

Jason's lips thinned. "I haven't stopped imagining the worst since you called."

She reached toward him, longing to ease his pain. When her head was a fraction of an inch away, she snatched it back. *I haven't the right to comfort him with more than words any-more.* The old sense of loss stabbed through her.

He rubbed a hand down his face in a gesture so familiar it caught at her heart. "I'm sorry I snapped at you. Chalk it up to shock and exhaustion, though it's no excuse."

"It's okay." The words came out in a cracked whisper. She pressed her lips together hard, unable to tear her gaze from his, wishing she could talk with him without remembering the way it felt to laugh with him and be in his arms.

"Mandy, we're back."

She whirled around at her sister Ellen's voice, swallowing hard and pasting on a smile. The back door slammed. A moment later, two girls raced across the room, dodging trees and gift items.

Six-year-old, chestnut-haired Bonnie threw her arms around Mandy's legs in her usual exuberant greeting. Mandy lifted the girl and gave her a hug. "Hello, Precious."

Bonnie's round arms tightened about Mandy's neck, and the gentle scent of baby shampoo filled Mandy's senses.

Eight-year-old Beth smiled, tilting her head, straight blond hair sliding over the shoulder of her red sweater. "Hi, Aunt Mandy."

Mandy slid her palm along the child's silky hair. "Hello, Sweetheart. What's for breakfast?"

Beth held up a white bag which emitted fast-food odors. "Sausage biscuits." A frown puckered her brow. "What happened to the tree?"

"A small accident. Nothing that can't be fixed."

"Sorry it took us so long." Ellen's voice preceded her as she crossed the room, expertly dodging Christmas trappings while tugging off her leather gloves. "The place was packed, and—" She caught sight of the tree with its broken and smashed decorations. "What happened to—"

She stopped, gloves dangling from one hand, and stared at Jason with her mouth open.

Jason nodded brusquely. "Ellen."

"J. P."

Ellen sounds as breathless as I was when I first saw him, Mandy thought in amusement.

Ellen closed the few feet between herself and J. P., her shoulder-length, straight brown hair swinging. She reached to shake hands. "Hello, J. P. I'm sorry about your grandfather. All my hopes and prayers are for his recovery."

"Thanks."

His gaze shifted from Ellen and rested on Bonnie, who still clung to Mandy's neck. Mandy noticed his puzzled look and remembered he wouldn't recognize the girls. Resting a hand on Beth's shoulder, she said, "You remember Ellen's daughter, Beth, don't you?"

He smiled at the shy, slender girl. "I remember. You were only a few months old when I last saw you."

Beth blushed and stared at him soberly.

"This is J. P.," Ellen told her. "Seth and Tillie's grandson."

Beth kept staring, not smiling.

His glance slid to the girl in Mandy's arms.

"This is Bonnie," Mandy said.

"Hello, Bonnie."

The girl burrowed her face into Mandy's neck at Jason's intense gaze. Why had his voice cracked when he greeted Bonnie? Mandy wondered. Was he thinking of the children they'd talked of having one day? Her stomach tightened painfully at the memory of the once-shared dream.

Ellen settled onto a backless stool beside the counter. "Is someone going to tell me why that Christmas tree looks like it belongs to Scrooge?"

Mandy shifted Bonnie to her other hip. "In a minute. We mustn't keep Jason. He hasn't seen his grandfather yet."

Mandy cringed inwardly at the look Ellen shot her. She could tell Ellen wasn't fooled by her polite dismissal of Jason.

"Of course," Ellen said smoothly. "Do give Seth our love, J. P. Tell him we'll bring the girls around to see him as soon as the hospital allows."

"I'll do that." He opened the door, then looked back, his gaze shifting between Mandy and Bonnie. "I'll talk to you later, Mandy."

She nodded. The tone beneath his simple statement raised havoc inside her. Would he demand a more complete explanation of why she'd leased this barn? Would he want her to give it up? Wait until he heard she lived above the shop.

Ellen pulled a biscuit from the bag. "All right, tell all."

Mandy set Bonnie down and knelt to pick up the crushed ornaments. "There's nothing to tell. Jason arrived at the farmhouse expecting to find Grandma Tillie. When he didn't, he stopped here, looking for her or some news about Grandpa Seth."

"That's all you two talked about? Grandpa Seth? After all these years? There were no sparks? No arguments? No kisses?"

"Kisses?" Beth was suddenly all eyes and ears.

"No kisses," Mandy told Ellen and Beth firmly. "Beth, will you and Bonnie help me pick up these nosegays? Watch out for broken pieces from the dolls' heads."

The girls joined her.

"You're avoiding me, Mandy Wells," Ellen charged.

"There's nothing to tell. Besides, I thought you'd given up on men."

"For me, not for you."

Mandy looked pointedly at the old schoolhouse clock on the wall above the counter. "You'll be late for work if you don't leave this minute, and I've got to feed the girls and get this mess cleaned up before I open for business."

Ellen slid off the stool. "All right, but you can't avoid me forever. I'll be back for your story at five-thirty. If the girls are too much trouble, make them take a nap—or pretend to take a nap."

"Mo–o–om," the girls chorused in indignation.

"Bye." Ellen headed toward the back door.

I won't be urging naps on the girls today, Mandy thought. Watching them, cleaning up the mess, and waiting on customers should keep her mind off Jason. Sunny October Saturdays always brought lots of people to the mountains and customers to the Christmas store.

She should be an expert at keeping her mind off Jason by now. It had taken years to get over him. *No, that's not accurate. It's taken years to get used to the pain of living without him in my life.* Still, she knew they couldn't make a marriage work, not as long as he insisted on living his father's dream instead of his own.

"Aunt Mandy." Bonnie tugged at the sleeve of Mandy's sweater. "Aren't you goin' to help us clean up?"

"Of course, Precious. I was just thinking about all we must do today."

"Looked like you were daydreaming." Beth glanced up from the floor with a crushed nosegay in her hand. "Mom says daydreaming is a waste of time."

Mandy didn't agree, but she didn't believe in going against her sister's parenting. Besides, this time, maybe Ellen was right. Instead of daydreaming, she should be praying for Jason.

She knew what was ahead for him. She'd seen Grandpa Seth only an hour ago when she'd dropped off Grandma Tillie. A monitor and IVs were attached to the dear, rugged, usually blustery old man lying in the hospital bed. Her heart ached, wishing she could spare Jason the shock of seeing his grandfather that way.

But all she could do was pray for Jason—and hurt with him for what he was going through.

three

Jason headed up the hill toward the car, his shiny black wing tips crunching through fallen leaves on the gravel drive. The sharp scent of dying leaves and earthy scent of loam in the nearby woodlands filled his senses. Songs of birds greeting the morning were a sharp contrast to the traffic sounds that usually surrounded him this time of day.

His grandparents' two-story white frame house with its dark green shutters nestled against the mountain and rose above the black rental car. High-backed oak rocking chairs sat on the porch that ran the width of the house, inviting him to "set a spell."

Jason scanned the view the house had looked out upon for 130 years. The mountains rolled away, ridge after ridge of rich autumn color with lazy fog drifting between them. Orderly rows of blue spruce and Fraser firs, the best Christmas trees grown, covered most of his grandfather's mountain. He loved those trees. Fear gnawed at him despite Mandy's assurances. Would his grandfather ever return to this place?

He turned his back on the tranquil scene and slid into the rental car. *The mountain's peace is an illusion,* he thought as he started down the mountain road toward town.

On top of his fear for his grandfather, he had to face his feelings for Mandy: beautiful, sweet, delightful, maddening Mandy. "Meddlin' Mandy," he'd teasingly called her, for her habit of involving herself in others' lives. Why hadn't his grandparents told him they'd leased the barn to her?

Bonnie was the spitting image of Mandy. The same unusually dark green eyes wide with permanent wonder beneath a spray of ridiculously long lashes, the same round face with the smallest sprinkling of freckles across her nose and beneath her eyes, the same silky hair the cinnamon color of acorns that fell from the tree in his grandparents' yard in autumn.

Pain coiled inside him. When had Mandy married? With other women, Bonnie might have been the result of a relationship outside marriage, but not with Mandy. Mandy believed in intimacy only within marriage. He believed the same, but it had been mighty hard to keep his hands from roaming during the years they'd dated.

He'd felt like he'd been hit in the gut with a sledgehammer when he saw Bonnie and realized Mandy was married. *What did you expect—that Mandy would sit around the mountains growing old, waiting for you to return?*

Deep in his heart, that's exactly what he'd expected, he grudgingly realized. He hadn't admitted it to himself before, but the surety that she could no more love another man enough to marry him than Jason could another woman had lived in his heart.

The child looked about six years old. Mandy couldn't have waited long after they broke up to marry. The pain in his chest twisted tighter.

She'd given her heart to someone else, and Gramps lay in a hospital bed trying to recover from a heart attack, he thought, turning into the hospital parking lot. Life couldn't get much bleaker. The takeover negotiations would have been a picnic compared to this.

Jason asked at the desk for his grandfather's room. A nurse directed him to ICU. The halls seemed hushed, filled with smells of disinfectants and medicines that spoke loudly of this being a place of death and healing.

His grandmother wasn't in the waiting area. Another nurse, middle-aged with red hair, directed him to the room. "Even family is allowed only a few minutes with the patient every couple hours," she warned.

Jason stopped with his palm against the door, closed his eyes, and pressed his lips tightly together. *Help me, Lord.* He was accustomed to facing wealthy, powerful men, helping them win in takeovers or mergers of mind-boggling dollar amounts—or helping them lose, depending on which side of the table they were seated. He'd never experienced the cold chills and dread he did now, facing his grandfather gravely ill, facing the fear in his grandmother's eyes, and knowing he couldn't make things better for either of them.

Jason took a deep breath and pushed the door open.

Only one bed stood in the room. On it lay an old man, his white hair and trim beard blending in with the pillowcase.

Jason shoved down the panic that swept through his chest at the sight of the tubes attached to his grandfather. Several IVs dripped drugs into his body. A steady *beep, beep* brought Jason's gaze to electrodes attached to Gramps's chest, connecting him to the monitor that watched his heart to catch any irregular beats. At least at the moment, the monitor wasn't off to the races or showing a flat line.

Gramps lay with his eyes closed. Gram held one of his hands in both her own, her gaze not leaving his face. Her long, thin frame was tensed, as though she was willing her own strength to become part of her husband. Neither noticed Jason's arrival.

He tried to say hello. His throat might as well have been glued shut. He swallowed. "Hello, Gram."

She whirled in her chair, still holding her husband's hand. Jason's heart clenched. Wrinkles had covered her face for as many years as he could remember, but until now she hadn't looked old and beaten. "Thank God, you made it."

The barely suppressed panic in her voice sent terror spiraling through him. Did she mean thank God he'd made it before Gramps died?

"You came." Gramps's voice was stronger than Jason expected, still a deep friendly growl. But the old man's smile was weak, and his pale blue eyes shrouded in pain—or fright.

Jason smiled, trying to ignore the fear inside. "Where else would I be, Gramps?"

"S'pose Tillie here went and called you. Made it sound like

I was halfway to the other side."

Gram's backbone straightened beneath her dark green sweat suit. "Course I called him. And you were more than halfway to the other side, Seth Kramer. If it weren't for Mandy helping me get you here, and for our prayers and Doctor Monroe—" She choked up.

Mandy had helped save his grandfather's life, Jason realized. Gratitude and guilt fought for supremacy. He should have been the one there for Gramps. Jason struggled to focus. Time for self-pity later. He shook his head, still smiling. "Womenfolk. Take credit for everything."

Gramps chuckled weakly. The chuckle turned into a cough, and pain creased his face.

Jason leaned forward. "Are you all right?"

He nodded. "Have a little pain in my chest, but Doc says that's not unusual."

Jason glanced at the monitor. It bleeped away, steady as a metronome. He breathed a sigh of relief.

The red-haired nurse entered. "You need to let the patient rest now." She held the door open while Gram kissed Gramps's cheek.

Jason slipped an arm around her shoulders. They felt as bony as always, but unlike normal, they trembled. He squeezed her reassuringly, then patted his grandfather's hand. "See you later."

"I'm glad you're here, Jason."

Gramps became a blur through Jason's sudden unshed tears. "Me too. I love you, Gramps."

Jason's thoughts raced as he and Gram stepped into the hall. He wanted to ask so many questions: What was Gramps's prognosis? Had he had any more attacks? Had the attack been mild or massive? Had the doctor performed any tests? Was the doctor still considering surgery or angioplasty?

He didn't know whether he dared ask Gram any of the questions racing through his mind. In spite of her tender heart, she'd always faced life's troubles with the sturdiness of a mountain. Now she seemed about to collapse. She paced the hall, her arms clutched tightly over her chest. Was she trying to keep from screaming with the pain and fear?

At least Mandy had been there for Gram and Gramps until he arrived. Warmth flooded his chest in bittersweet gratitude. If Mandy had married him and moved to New York like he'd wanted her to do, she wouldn't have been there yesterday afternoon.

When Dr. Monroe—a middle-aged man with pepper-and-salt hair and a calm, competent manner custom-made for reassuring patients and kin—came by, Jason questioned him with a thoroughness learned from tenaciously tracking down every pertinent fact in his business dealings. After fifteen minutes, Jason felt convinced of his grandfather's relative safety for the moment, and the doctor moved on.

Gram said, "They won't let us see Seth again for almost an hour. He needs his rest, they say. I think he needs the people he loves more, but the doctor and nurses are firm about the rule."

"They want him to recover too, Gram, and they've a lot more experience with heart attacks than we do. Let's go to the cafeteria. You probably haven't eaten yet today."

Gram insisted she wasn't hungry, but Jason plied her with cinnamon rolls and decaffeinated coffee. Not the best nutrition, but good for calming the nerves, and they needed that.

"If you stopped by the farm, I guess you saw the Christmas barn." Gram looked down at her coffee cup, appearing a tad ashamed.

"Yes, and Mandy." Jason felt a sliver of satisfaction at her discomfort.

"You talked to her?"

"For a few minutes."

She sighed. "S'pose we should have told you 'bout Mandy's store months ago."

"Would have been nice." He kept his voice even. This was no time for the full-scale bawling out he'd like to give her and Gramps.

She stirred her cold coffee. "We kept waiting for the right time. We convinced ourselves to wait until you came home for a visit. Then this happened." One bony shoulder lifted the sweatshirt in a shrug as if to say, "and you know the rest."

Guilt swamped him—again. Her voice held no hint of reproach, but he couldn't pretend she and Gramps weren't aware his last visit home was last Christmas. He'd told his prickling conscience the demands of building a career justified his absence, but he knew better.

"How is your job going?"

He was glad for the change of subject. To try to keep their minds away from their fears, he chatted on about his work and life in New York while they walked back to the visitors' lounge on the ICU floor.

Finally the red-haired nurse told them they could visit Gramps for a few more minutes.

"Heart surgery?" Gramps was asking Dr. Monroe when they entered the room. "Are you sure I need that? I mean, the heart attack didn't kill me."

"The next one might. The valves at the back of your heart are blocked. Without the bypass surgery, if the next attack doesn't take you out, the following one will. It's only a matter of time."

"Can't it wait, Doc? Our busiest season is just starting."

Gram hurried to the bedside. "Seth Kramer, how dare you talk about business when your life is at stake."

"If I'm going to live, I need to support us, don't I? With Ted gone, there isn't another man I trust to take us through the Christmas season. If we miss this season, we don't make any money until this time next year."

Ted had worked with Gramps all Jason's life until just a few months ago when Ted had died of cancer. Eight other men worked full-time at the farm, but Gramps didn't trust any of them the way he had Ted. Jason knew if Ted were still alive, Gramps would have followed the doctor's advice. Without Ted. . .

Gram's pointed chin jutted out. "I can run things this one year."

"You handle the paperwork side of the business fine, Tillie. And the wreaths and roping too. Better than fine. But you don't know diddly-squat about the rest of the business."

"Foolish old man."

"Hold it." Dr. Monroe lifted both hands. "Arguing about business isn't going to help your heart, Seth."

Jason spoke up. "Nothing to argue about anyway. I'm taking a leave of absence from the firm. I'll run the Christmas tree farm through the busy season."

Gramps's frown deepened. "You can't do a thing like that, Boy. You've got your own career to think about. What would happen to that important takeover you're working on?"

"Others in the firm can handle it. I'll keep in touch by phone and E-mail."

"You haven't worked at the farm since your college days. Things have changed."

Jason saw the hope growing in the older man's face in spite of his protests. "You can explain the changes to me. I'll talk with the other growers. We'll work it out together."

Gramps closed his eyes. "It's too much to ask of you."

"You're not asking. I'm offering. I want to do it."

Gramps studied Jason's face. Jason met his gaze evenly. He'd do anything in his power to increase his grandfather's chances of recovery. Neal wouldn't be happy about the leave of absence, but he'd go along with it. Jason knew his worth to the company.

"You're sure about this, Boy?"

"I'm sure."

"Welcome aboard." Gramps lifted his hand a short way above the mattress. Jason met it with his own.

Dr. Monroe breathed an exaggerated sigh of relief, bringing nervous laughter from them all. "Now that that's resolved, I suggest you two let Seth rest awhile."

Back at the visitors' area, Gram grasped one of Jason's

hands in both her own. "Thank you."

She looked more relaxed than when he'd arrived, and her shoulders no longer trembled. *At least my offer to help with the farm gave her a measure of peace,* Jason thought. He pulled her close in a hug and planted a kiss on her wrinkled cheek. She wasn't a woman who ordinarily inspired protective gestures. She was almost as tall as he and slender. Rangy, Gramps affectionately described her.

The large round clock on the wall read eleven o'clock. Only nineteen hours since he'd received the call about his grandfather's heart attack. Nineteen hours in which his whole life had changed. Nineteen hours in which his own heart hadn't stopped hurting, fearing, or praying.

God willing, Gramps would come through the bypass surgery with flying colors, but how long before Jason and Gram could look at Gramps without wondering when another attack might come?

Gram pushed herself out of his arms and went to stare out the window.

Jason pulled his cell phone from his suit-coat pocket and punched the power button. The battery was dead. He grimaced. "I'd better call New York and tell them my plans, Gram. I'll be back in a few minutes."

"All right, Jason."

He started down the hall toward the public phones he'd noticed earlier. He was growing accustomed to hearing himself called Jason again. At work, everyone called him J. P., for Jason Peter. His father had given him the nickname years ago, saying with a grin that the initials were good for a man in finance, the same initials as J. P. Morgan and J. P. Getty. Only his grandparents and Mandy never called him J. P.

Mandy. A shiver reverberated through him at the memory of his name on her lips this morning. He'd hungered to hear her whisper his name for so long, but in love, not shock.

For the foreseeable future he was back in the mountains he loved, the mountains he'd forced himself to leave, doing the work he'd loved and left as well, watching and worrying over Gramps.

And living on the same farm as Mandy and her Christmas barn. The same Mandy who'd lived in his dreams for eight years, preventing him from giving his heart to another woman—not that he hadn't tried.

The picture of Mandy holding Bonnie flashed through his mind, and pain tore sharply through him. Mandy wasn't the same person after all. She was a mother. And that meant she was a wife.

Nineteen hours ago he'd thought himself in control of his life. He was good at his profession. He'd learned to live without the mountains and Mandy and was used to the dull pain those losses left inside him.

The toughest months of his life were just ahead. "I never needed Your help more, Lord," he whispered, lifting the pay phone from its cradle.

four

I was sure right about that phone call to Neal, Jason thought a few days later as he walked from the groves to the farmhouse. Neal's anger and frustration had heated the phone lines but hadn't changed Jason's mind.

He'd been too busy to worry about Neal while working the trees, but he'd need to make his daily check-in call before too long. Maybe he could work it in during the supper break.

Half an hour wasn't nearly enough time to eat and renew himself for another round of work that evening. Jason had thought his daily jog and workout kept him in shape, but only determination not to be shown up by the locals and migrant workers had kept him going through the long days of physical labor, cutting trees and loading them into the binder and then onto trucks.

Mouthwatering odors met him when he entered the old kitchen. He sniffed appreciatively. Roast beef. "I'm home, Gram," he called. "Supper sure smells good."

"She isn't here."

"Mandy." He whirled toward the dining room door. Mandy wore one of Gram's old terry-cloth aprons over a white shirt and jeans. His insides tightened with the pain of knowing she was unattainable. He felt too tired to fight his attraction for her. The knowledge sharpened his voice. "Where's Gram?"

Mandy pushed her hands into the apron pockets. He saw her make fists, bunching the material. "Grandma Tillie is still at the hospital. She asked me to make you dinner." She waved a hand toward an orange slow cooker on the wooden counter. "Roast beef, browned potatoes, and carrots. I hope you're hungry."

"Hungry like a bear, but you don't need to look after me.

I'm quite accustomed to taking care of myself. Gram forgets that sometimes."

"She doesn't forget. She cares about you. She knows how long the days are working the trees and wants to make things easier for you."

He hated the hurt-animal look his attitude had put in her eyes. "Sorry. Guess I've lived so long by myself that I've forgotten what family is like."

She removed an ironstone platter from the white, wooden standing cupboard, then forked the roast and vegetables onto the platter. "The gravy should be ready about the time you finish washing up."

He looked down at his pine-tar-covered hands and grimaced. Leaving his heavy boots beside the door and hanging his jacket on a peg above them, he walked to the sink. While washing up, he watched Mandy stir gravy in a cast-iron skillet. She didn't look much older than when they'd dated. She'd spent lots of time at the farm with him then. It seemed natural to see her here. "Will you join me for dinner, Mandy?"

Her startled gaze darted to him.

No wonder his suggestion surprised her, considering the way he'd snapped at her earlier. Before he could let himself change his mind he wheedled, "You're the one who made the meal. You deserve the pleasure of eating it."

Her cheeks dimpled. "Assuming it is a pleasure. You haven't tasted it yet."

He grinned. "I'll take my chances."

She continued stirring the gravy while she bit her bottom lip and looked as if she were debating his invitation. It rankled him that she hesitated. He whipped a blue-checked towel from the wooden towel rack above the sink. "Look, don't think you need to stay."

"I don't. I was thinking about Grandma Tillie. I promised to pick her up."

"Gram won't leave the hospital for hours yet, even though

Gramps is out of ICU now."

"There's the store too. I need to check on things before going to the hospital."

Was it his imagination, or did she sound panicky? Did she find his company so unpleasant she couldn't share a few minutes with him over dinner? "I need to be back in the fields in twenty-five minutes. You wouldn't have to endure my company long." He threw the towel down on the counter.

"I didn't say—"

"You didn't have to." He heaved a sigh and ran a hand over his face. "Look, you have every right to leave. You've done more than enough making the meal." He forced a smile. "I plan to enjoy every bite."

"Jason. . ."

He yanked out a chair. Its legs scraped across the black-and-white linoleum. "You've given more time than our family could expect already."

"I was glad to make supper." She set the platter down on the table, followed by two plates.

His heart skipped a beat, then raced on. She'd decided to join him.

"I'm not talking only about the meal." He tried to keep his voice casual. "You've spent a lot of time chauffeuring Gram back and forth to the hospital and visiting Gramps."

"They're friends." Mandy's eyes flashed. She settled her fists on her too-round-for-fashion, apron-clad hips. "People might not help friends in New York, but here it's still considered the proper thing to do."

Laughter rumbled in his chest. He leaned back, balancing the chair on its hind legs. "I haven't seen you spit fire like that since I sneaked the black snake into English lit class."

"And scared poor Professor Potts out of her wits."

"It was just a little black snake. Couldn't hurt her any."

"Especially since she was standing on her desk, screaming bloody murder."

He shrugged. "Class needed some excitement."

"English lit was an elective. If you didn't like it, why did you take it?"

"You were in the class."

Her eyes widened. She glanced away from him and sat down. As she bowed her head, he did the same and said a silent grace.

When he looked back up, she was lifting her fork. "A snake, Jason. Honestly." A smile teased at the edge of her full lips, then grew. "You were impossible back then." Her voice dropped to a soft level that set his pulse racing.

He shrugged and picked up his own fork, hoping she couldn't see how much she'd affected him. "I wasn't impossible. I was just a typical college boy who didn't know whether a certain girl liked him and wasn't very sophisticated in his attempts to get her attention."

"You were never typical."

Her grin turned his insides to Jell-O.

"Besides," she continued, her attention focused on cutting her meat, "you had nothing to worry about concerning that girl's affections."

He rested his forearms on the table and stared at her. "If that's true, why are you living in the mountains when I'm living in New York?"

Her gaze jerked to his. He saw disbelief and pain in her eyes.

His question hadn't been a question at all. He saw she recognized it for the accusation he'd meant it.

"You know the answer to that." Her voice held no hint of the defense he'd expected. "I—"

"You're right." He lifted one palm to stop her. His voice rose in anger. "Forget it." He didn't truly want to hear again that she hadn't loved him enough to marry him and leave the mountains.

Mandy pushed her chair back and stood. "I need to get back to the store."

"Mandy, I'm sorry. I—"

She hurried to the door, grabbed a brown corduroy coat

from the peg beside his jacket, and left. The door slammed behind her.

Jason sighed and rubbed his eyes with a thumb and index finger. "Don't know how to handle women any better than I did when I was a college kid."

Loneliness twisted through him. He shoved away his still-full plate.

five

The brass bells over the Christmas shop door announced another customer. The spicy scent of autumn leaves wafted inside on the October wind, reminding Mandy of the world outside the shop's constant holiday environment.

I should have put the closed sign on the door after the last customer left, Mandy thought. She glanced at the ornately carved cuckoo clock on the wall above the counter. Almost seven o'clock. At this rate she'd never get to the hospital to see Grandpa Seth and pick up Grandma Tillie.

Her gaze shifted to the man who'd entered. Jason. Her heart missed a beat. She hadn't seen him since the roast beef meal two evenings earlier.

She knew from Grandma Tillie that Jason divided his time between visits to the hospital, work in the Christmas tree groves, and phone calls to his New York office. Mandy had left hot meals in the slow cooker the last couple days, but she'd carefully stayed away from the house when she expected him there.

Why was he here? He wore a cautious look. Likely he wondered what kind of welcome she'd give him after the other night. She wished he hadn't brought up the subject of their breakup. Obviously he planned to live in New York permanently. Neither of their goals had changed. So why bring up a subject that could only open old wounds?

Jason nodded a greeting, jammed his hands into the pockets of his stone-colored twill slacks, and began wandering around the shop.

Smothering a sigh of relief, she turned her attention back to the middle-aged woman with the gray-streaked black hair seated in the wheelchair, and the burly, brown-bearded man standing beside her.

A dozen Christmas cards with the look of hand-painted watercolors stretched across the counter. At one end lay a large painting of Seth and Tillie's mountainside home in winter.

"The cards are exquisite, Alma." Mandy touched the deckled edge of one. "My customers will love them."

A grin wreathed Alma's face. "I never thought I'd see my paintings outside my own home." She glanced up at the large man beside her. "Or my boy's home. I'd never have dared try sell them if not for you, Mandy."

"Thank your son." Mandy smiled at the man. He smiled shyly back. "He's the one who showed me your paintings. How could you keep such a talent secret?"

"Not hard when you're an invalid. People don't expect much from invalids." The words were said matter-of-factly, without self-pity.

"People will know they've been wrong when they see your cards and paintings."

"That they will," Tom Berry agreed.

"Tom's convinced other shops to carry my cards," Alma said proudly, "but not around here. I want your store to be the only place to offer them in this area."

"I take samples along on my selling trips," Tom explained. "Leaving next week on another. Last chance to get things into shops before Christmas. Most of the stores placed their orders six months ago."

"Tom?"

Mandy jumped at the sound of Jason's voice beside her.

Jason reached out a hand. "Tom Berry? I didn't recognize you until I heard your voice. Guess we've both changed a bit since we graduated from high school."

Tom shook Jason's hand. "Good to see you, J. P."

Although Jason was a good-sized man and as tall as Tom, he looked slender and small beside him, Mandy thought.

"How is your grandfather?" Alma asked.

Jason filled them in, accepted their best wishes for his grandfather, then turned his attention to the greeting cards.

"These are great. Your work, Tom?"

"My work," Alma corrected.

Shock registered in Jason's eyes. His glance fell to the hands lying useless in Alma's lap. "I didn't realize you painted."

Mandy wished she'd had a chance to tell Jason about Alma Berry's talent. She knew he hadn't meant to be rude.

"I hold the brush in my mouth." Alma's voice was as stiff as her chair. "It takes awhile, but I get the work done."

"And beautifully." Jason held one of the cards where the light could strike it better.

"For an invalid?" There was a quiet challenge in her question.

Jason met her gaze evenly. "For anyone. You have a true talent for catching the mountain's beauty."

"Thank you." Alma's voice relaxed.

His gaze slipped to the large painting. "My grandparents' farm."

The woman laughed. "I'm glad you recognize it."

"It's perfect." He turned to Tom. "So if you're not an artist, what do you do?"

"I'm an artist of sorts—a potter. Didn't take it up until after high school. Started out small, just doing local craft shows, but I'm doing pretty well at it now, thanks to this little lady." He nodded his massive head in Mandy's direction. "She managed a shop in Asheville. When she saw my work at a local craft show, she bought a few pieces for her shop. I never would have had the courage to try to sell to an upscale shop like that."

Mandy grinned at him. "I know talent when I see it, even if I can't create masterpieces myself. Now his work is in demand throughout the surrounding states," she told Jason.

"Haven't had the kind of success you've had, J. P." Tom's beard-surrounded grin showed he wasn't jealous.

Mandy thought Jason looked uncomfortable at Tom's comment. Jason's shoulders lifted his brown sweater in a shrug. "Everyone has their own definition of success."

Tom nodded. "Isn't that the truth."

Mandy studied Jason's face. Wasn't he happy with the life he'd worked so hard to build in New York, making his father's dream his own?

The brass bells jangled as Beth and Bonnie burst into the room, followed by Ellen. The girls saw the Berrys and dashed over, throwing themselves against Tom's trunklike legs. After he'd greeted them to their satisfaction, they turned to Alma, each standing on tiptoe to kiss the older woman's cheek.

They ignored Mandy and Jason. Mandy smiled. She knew the girls would greet her later. She was a fixture in their lives.

Beth grabbed one of Tom's arms with both hands. "Lift us up."

Bonnie grabbed the other arm. "Yes, lift us up."

"You two have grown so much, I might not be strong enough to lift you anymore."

Usually sober Beth giggled. "You're strong enough."

"Yes," Bonnie encouraged. "Lift us up."

"I'll try. Beth first. Hang on tight." He lifted his arm slowly. Beth swung from it, giggling so hard her face turned red. His own face showed the strain of her weight, but he lifted her until his arm reached shoulder height.

Mandy chanced a glance at Jason's face. Shock, then humor and admiration for Tom's strength showed plainly.

"Beth!" Ellen's cry brought Mandy's gaze to her. She'd forgotten Ellen hadn't seen the girls and Tom pull this stunt.

Ellen's exclamation caught Tom's attention too. He lowered Beth carefully to the floor.

Ellen grabbed Beth's shoulders. "That's no way to behave."

"But Tom always lifts us."

"That's right." Tom intervened.

"It's my turn." Bonnie tugged at Tom's hand.

Tom glanced at Ellen and lifted thick brown eyebrows in question.

Ellen grinned. "If you want to, go ahead, but don't blame me for the veins bulging in your neck and forehead."

His eyes twinkled. "Fair enough. Ready, Bonnie?"

Ellen watched Tom easily lift Bonnie, then turned to Mandy and asked whether the carpenter had shown up that day. He hadn't. "I'm about ready to repair that chest myself," Ellen said in disgust. "That's the fourth time he's promised to come and not shown."

"I'm pretty good at carpentry, Miss Ellen," Tom offered. "I'd be glad to help you out."

"We couldn't ask you to do that," Mandy protested. "Especially at this time of year. You're busy with your own work."

"I like doing something other than pottery. Relaxes me."

"Well, if you're sure. . . ," Ellen said, hesitating for his answer.

"Then it's settled." Tom nodded at Ellen. "If you'll show me what needs to be repaired, I'll know what tools to bring."

She led him to the loft, the girls following at Tom's heels.

Mandy was relieved to see Jason start about the room again, examining the trees and other decorations. Alma began a conversation again, but Mandy had difficulty following it. Instead her mind followed Jason.

Why had he come today? Did he have the same desire to talk with her that she had to talk with him? She'd heard a great deal about him through his grandparents over the last eight years, but she wanted to find out for herself if he was happy, if he'd found what he'd sought when he left her and the mountains for New York—whether it had been worth the cost of their love.

He stopped briefly at a teddy bear tree, at another tree covered with Scandinavian woven-wheat and red wooden ornaments, and yet at another with delicate, handblown glass balls.

He lingered longest at her favorite, a copy of the famous angel tree set up each year at the Metropolitan Museum of Art in New York. The tree was covered with copies of eighteenth-century angels and cherubs. A large crèche stood beneath the tree. Shepherds, kings on camels, and animals spread out among the rocks and moss surrounding the crèche. She watched Jason run a finger lightly along an angel's stiff, rose-colored gown.

Alma was eagerly explaining some detail of her paintings, but Mandy couldn't drag her attention back from Jason. Did he recall when they saw the original tree at the Met? The way they'd stood before it in hushed awe, holding hands, and afterward admitting they felt as though they'd been blessed with witnessing the closest thing possible to the actual night of Christ's birth? Her chest ached, suddenly too small to hold the emotion-charged memory.

Jason turned, his finger still on the angel's gown. His gaze met hers across the room. A bond bridged the distance between them. To Mandy it seemed tinged with regret for what they'd lost, filled with hope for forgiveness.

Abruptly, he turned his back to her, and the delicate bridge collapsed. Mandy blinked and took a shaky breath. Had she imagined it all? Or had he pulled back when he sensed what was happening between them, not ready even after eight years to forgive her for not marrying him?

She'd desperately wanted to marry him, but she'd always known she wanted to live in the mountains. Living in the city would be like a living death for her, the same as her beloved mountains would be a prison to a true city lover. It made no sense to begin a marriage with such a wall between them, but she hadn't been able to convince Jason of that.

She forced her attention back to Alma. Mandy lifted Alma's painting, admiring again the winter mountain scene. "I'd like to put this above the fireplace. What do you think?"

Alma's dark eyes sparkled. "Do you honestly believe it's worthy of such a prominent placement?"

"Quit begging for compliments," Mandy teased.

Alma shifted in her chair, a pleased smile on her face. "J. P., can you help Mandy with this painting?"

"I can hang it myself." Mandy wondered whether she actually paled at Alma's call. She didn't need Jason any closer to her. She was all too aware of his presence as it was.

Jason's glance met hers above the painting. "Where do you want it?"

"Over the fireplace." She started for the center of the room, carrying the painting.

Before following Mandy, Jason took time to turn Alma's chair so she could see the fireplace. "You let us know when we have it positioned just right, Alma," he said. "A painting should always be hung to please the artist."

Where did he come upon that bit of wisdom? He hadn't known much about art when they were dating. No telling how much he'd changed since they'd been together. It surprised Mandy to find how much it hurt to realize she no longer knew him inside and out.

But if she'd really known him inside and out back then, she'd have known he'd eventually leave her for a career in New York, instead of fooling herself into believing that deep inside, he wanted to stay in the mountains she loved—with her.

She set the picture down and pulled the overstuffed, red plaid footstool over to the hearth. Jason stepped on the stool and reached for the huge grapevine wreath above the mantel. Handing it to her, he said, "Give me the painting."

She steadied the painting as he took hold of it. Much of the painting's weight stayed in her hands, and she looked up at him. Why wasn't he taking it?

His gaze was riveted on her left hand. Had the grapevine scratched it without her noticing? She glanced down but saw nothing unusual and looked back, puzzled.

His questioning gaze shifted to hers. "You aren't wearing a wedding ring."

The accusation in his tone sent a warm wave up her neck. She was glad he hadn't spoken loud enough for Alma to hear over the Christmas music. "There's no law that a thirty-year-old woman has to be married."

"Is something wrong with the painting?" Alma called.

Jason lifted the painting from Mandy's hands. "Nothing at

all," he assured the artist. "Just wanted to be sure I didn't snag Mandy's hands with the wire."

Mandy wished she and Jason were alone so she could ask him why he'd thought she was married. His question intensified her already-overactive awareness of him. They were so close she could hear his breathing.

By the time Jason had the picture hung to Alma's satisfaction, Tom, Ellen, and the girls were down from the loft. Tom showed Jason a tree decorated with Tom's slender pottery ornaments, and then the Berrys prepared to leave. Ellen and the girls went out to the car with them.

When Jason and Mandy were alone, Jason said, "The girls certainly like Tom."

"Tom and Grandpa Seth are the only two men those girls trust anymore." It felt safer talking about them than herself, Mandy thought, but safe wasn't always the best. She took a deep breath and plunged in. "Who told you I was married?"

Deep red color crept up his neck. He lifted his shoulders in a shrug. "I. . .assumed. Are you divorced?"

"No." Her answer came out louder than she'd intended. With an effort, she lowered her voice. "I never married. What made you think. . . ?"

His gaze darted away. His face scrunched into a wince. "Bonnie. She's the spitting image of you, and I didn't think you would. . .not without being married." His voice dropped significantly on the last words.

Did he think she'd abandoned her values after they broke up? "Bonnie is Ellen's daughter."

Jason's eyes widened, then begged forgiveness. "I'm afraid I've put my foot in it."

She turned her back and fiddled with a Victorian ornament on a tree to prevent his seeing the hurt in her eyes.

He rested a hand on her arm. His touch sent a charge blazing through her. She heard his breath catch. Had he been as affected by their touch as she was?

"Mandy, I'm sorry. I didn't think you'd abandoned your

values or your faith. I thought you were married because Bonnie looks so much like you, and I knew you wouldn't sleep with anyone outside marriage."

The huskiness in his voice assured her of his sincerity, but his voice combined with his touch caused dangerous warnings of desire to dance along her nerve endings. She stepped back, and his hand fell away.

The only sound in the room was a harpsichord rendition of "Hark, the Herald Angels Sing." It didn't hide the tension between them. Jason cleared his throat. "I didn't put much hope in Ellen and Zach's marriage lasting, but I guess Beth and Bonnie are proof that it has."

Mandy shook her head, glad for a topic less personal than her own choices about marriage and sex. "Zach left her and the girls last year. The divorce was final last month. He believes he's meant for better things than managing a small-town clothing store. He's in California. He's written a screenplay and feels he can sell it better face-to-face than through the mail."

"Couldn't he let an agent handle the selling? He could support himself here, living here with his family, while someone else hawks the script."

"That's too sensible. You know Zach. Besides, he evidently feels a family is a liability to his dreams."

He scowled. "I always felt guilty for introducing him to Ellen."

"You hadn't much choice, as I recall. Zach crashed the pizza party that night and demanded an introduction to Ellen. Besides, you couldn't have kept them apart. Remember how the air between them sizzled?"

"I remember. They were married only. . .what. . .three months later?"

His intense gaze and strained voice made her wonder if he was recalling that he'd told her how, in spite of his doubts about Ellen and Zach's marriage, he was jealous of them and wished it were he and Mandy marrying instead. The memory made it difficult for her to concentrate.

"Uh, yes, three months. Look, did you come here for something special? I told Grandma Tillie I'd stop at the hospital to see Grandpa Seth tonight and bring her home."

"Actually, Gram asked me to come down."

Irrationally, his comment sent disappointment burning through her. In spite of telling herself for years that it was for the best that they hadn't married, and even though they'd parted angry the other evening, part of her had hoped he'd come tonight because he couldn't stay away from her.

"I brought Gram home," he went on. "She's already asleep. She wanted to stay at the hospital all night. She hasn't said so, but I know she's frightened about Gramps's bypass surgery tomorrow. Gramps told her he's tired and will rest more easily knowing she's at home getting some sleep. Besides." He grinned almost conspiratorially. "He says he'll go into surgery more positive tomorrow if he knows she's at the hospital praying for him, not asleep because she's been up all night worrying about him."

Mandy couldn't help smiling back. "That sounds like Grandpa Seth. I wish I'd made it up there to talk with him tonight."

"You can talk with him after the surgery."

His voice trembled only slightly, but enough for her to recognize his words were a defense against his own fear.

She nodded. "Of course."

Her heart smarted. He looked so tired. She wanted to draw his head against her shoulder, caress his hair, and whisper words of comfort. Instead she sat down, folding one leg beneath her in the wing chair, putting further distance between them.

Jason cleared his throat. "I also wanted to apologize for the other night." He dug his hands into his slacks' pockets, then pulled his hands out and sat on the edge of the wing chair opposite her. "I spoke out of turn. The past is past. Since I'm going to be around for the next couple months, I'm hoping we can be friends."

She nodded. "Sure." On the surface they could be friends, but the past wasn't behind them, not when he hadn't forgiven her for not marrying him, not when she still longed to share life with him.

He must want to put it behind him, she thought with a sinking feeling in her stomach. *Even though during our disagreement he'd sounded as though he wished we hadn't broken up. He found out tonight I'm not married, and instead of saying he'd like to try again, he's telling me he wants to put the past behind us.* She bit back the regret burning within her.

The door flew open. Beth's and Bonnie's giggles interrupted them. The girls raced each other across the room and threw themselves against the arms of Mandy's chair.

"I won," Beth called.

Bonnie shook her head until her curls swirled against her round, flushed cheeks. "No, I won."

"No, you didn't."

"Yes, I did, didn't I, Aunt Mandy?"

Both were giggling so hard they could barely challenge each other. Mandy gave each a quick one-armed hug. "I declare the race an official tie."

"Anyone for hot chocolate?" Ellen asked, taking up last place in the newcomers' race. "I need something to settle these two down before they go to bed."

"Bed?"

"We're not ready for bed."

Jason stood. "I should be going."

"Don't leave on our account," Ellen protested. "Mandy and I can talk whenever we want. I'll take the girls up to get their pajamas on, and then we'll be back down for hot chocolate."

Mandy and Jason watched the three climb the open wooden staircase to the loft.

Jason's gaze wandered to the fireplace with its mountain river rocks reaching to the beamed roof. "I don't remember the fireplace."

"I had it built."

"Nice." Jason walked to the hearth, staring into the embers.

Mandy listened to the embers crackling and bursting and felt the pain of the thick, uncomfortable silence between herself and Jason.

It was a relief when Bonnie came bounding down the stairs, a huge brown teddy bear in her arms. Leaning her head against Mandy's knees, she studied Jason with her wide-eyed gaze.

He smiled at the girl, and Mandy thought his face truly relaxed for the first time that night. She'd always loved watching him with children; he so thoroughly enjoyed them.

"Great Barbie doll nightgown," Jason said.

"Thank you," Bonnie answered primly.

"Why do you keep your pajamas upstairs here? Are you and your sister going to have a sleepover under the Christmas trees?"

Bonnie shook her head, her brown curls bouncing. "No. We're goin' to sleep upstairs in our bed."

Jason frowned, looking puzzled. "Your bed is upstairs?"

"Of course, Silly. We live here."

Jason's eyebrows shot up. "You live here?"

Mandy touched the tip of her tongue to suddenly dry lips.

"Who lives here with you, Bonnie?" Jason's voice held a cautious note, as though afraid he already knew the answer.

"Mommy, Beth." Bonnie nodded once for each name. Mandy held her breath as the girl nodded a third time. "And Aunt Mandy."

Jason's gaze darted to Mandy's.

She spread her arms and grinned, hoping he couldn't see how her courage wavered. "Surprise."

six

"A surprise, indeed," Jason agreed with what he congratulated himself was a good degree of calm considering the jolt he'd just received. "Amazing that you, Gram, and Gramps all forgot to mention that little detail. From the mouths of babes."

Bonnie frowned. "What's that mean? 'From the mouth of babes.' "

"That one is all yours," Mandy challenged Jason.

He knew what she meant. No six year old wanted to be called a baby. "It's a very old saying," he explained. "It means children say wise things."

Bonnie's eyes sparkled. "Children like me?"

"Just like you," Jason assured her. He sat down with his elbows on his knees and his fingers linked.

Bonnie studied him soberly, crushing her beige teddy bear against the pink-clad blond Barbie on her nightgown. "Would you like to see my teddy bear?"

"Sure."

She stepped cautiously to the coffee table and handed the bear across.

Jason examined it soberly. Its curly tan fur was well worn, and the red-and-green ribbon around its neck looked like it had been chewed, most likely by Bonnie's tiny white teeth. "A very handsome bear. What's his name?"

"Teddy."

"Very appropriate."

"What's 'propie. . . , 'propie. . . ?"

"Appropriate," he repeated slowly. "It means it's just right."

Her grin widened, and she stuck out her stomach in pride.

A movement caught his eye, and he looked up to see Ellen sit down in the wing chair opposite Mandy. Beth leaned against her mother's knees, her hair, as blond as her negligent father's, brushed behind her ears in a smooth sweep. Her nightgown featured the dark-haired princess from *Aladdin*.

When Beth noticed him looking at her, she slipped the tip of her little finger between her lips and turned her head partially away, as if wanting to hide. *Shy thing,* he thought. He winked at her and felt pleasantly rewarded he'd surprised her into a smile, even though she instantly retreated behind her sober face and measuring eyes.

"Ready for your hot chocolate, girls?" Mandy asked, rising. At the girls' assurance that they were indeed ready, she went to fill their cups.

Jason absently bounced the bear up and down on one knee.

"Teddy likes 'to market, to market,' " Bonnie informed him.

"What's that?"

"You know. Teddy rides to market on your leg, only he's really riding a horse, of course."

"Give me a hint how it starts."

She heaved such a huge sigh of disgust that he bit back a laugh. " 'To market, to market,' " she began, waving her hands like a philharmonic conductor, " 'to fetch a skein of wool.' "

"I remember. 'Uphill, downhill, fall in a hole,' " he finished with her, bouncing the bear high on his knee, then plunging the bear almost to the floor.

Bonnie clapped, laughing. "Do it again."

"We don't want to get Teddy too excited so close to bedtime."

Bonnie accepted the bear without further quibbling. But it was Mandy's chuckle at Jason's diplomatic argument that was music to his ears as she returned with cups of chocolate with bobbing marshmallow clouds for the girls. When he glanced at Ellen and Beth, Beth was smiling too, until she saw him looking at her.

Bonnie leaned against the coffee table, concentrating heavily on Teddy's face, where her tiny fingers tugged at one black button eye. "Mr. J. P., are you a daddy?"

"No."

"Why not?"

"I was never blessed with nice girls like you and your sister."

Bonnie looked at him, her smiling glance almost shy, obviously pleased with his answer.

Beth wasn't pleased. "Our daddy doesn't feel blessed to be a daddy. He left us."

Ellen's arms circled Beth's waist, but the girl stood stiff, watching for Jason's reaction.

He felt Bonnie watching him too, as well as Mandy. What could he say that wouldn't be dishonest or cruel to the little girls? Anger built inside him, sweeping up through his chest. How could any man leave his children? "It's hard to learn to live without your dad, isn't it? I had to learn to live without mine too."

"Did he divorce you and your mom?" Beth asked. Curiosity and caution mingled in her blue eyes.

His heart caught at her belief her father had divorced not only Ellen but the girls. "No. When I was a teenager, my dad died in an automobile accident."

Beth and Bonnie stared at him, wide-eyed. The fire spit and crackled from tree sap while the girls absorbed what he'd said.

"I know lots of kids at school whose dads left them like ours," Beth said slowly, "but I don't know anyone whose dad is dead."

"Did it hurt you when he died?" Bonnie rubbed her Barbie-covered chest. "In here?"

He nodded. "Yes, it hurt me a lot in there."

"Does it hurt still?"

"Sometimes, but not as bad as it used to."

Bonnie's chubby fingers pulled at the bear's black button eye. "I still hurt lots when I think about my daddy."

Beth pushed at her hair and lifted her pointed chin defiantly. "I don't hurt. I hate him."

"Honey," Ellen protested, "you know you don't hate your father."

She tried to pull the girl closer, but Beth pushed free. "Yes, I do."

"I think it's time for bed," Ellen said softly. Jason saw tears glittering in her eyes.

"I haven't finished my hot chocolate," Bonnie protested.

"Take it upstairs with you."

"I'm sorry, Ellen." Jason spoke quietly. "I didn't mean to disturb the girls."

Her eyes looked old and tired. "You didn't say anything wrong. The fault lies elsewhere."

He noticed she didn't say where. Was she one of those gallant mothers who never said anything negative about her ex-husband in front of his children? Difficult task, to put it mildly, but he admired her for it.

Ellen stood. "Come on, girls, let's get going."

Mandy leaned forward to give Bonnie a hug that was strenuously returned. Jason's heart constricted at the sight, at the thought of what it would be like if Mandy was saying good night to their child, his and Mandy's. If they'd had a little girl, would she look like Bonnie, like a miniature Mandy?

"Good night, Mr. J. P." Bonnie's round brown eyes gleamed in a smile repeated on her lips, but she didn't offer to hug him.

"Good night, Bonnie. And you don't need to call me mister, since we're friends."

She grinned.

Beth hugged Mandy with only slightly less reserve than her sister. Standing safely by Mandy's chair, Beth gave Jason a small wave and a smaller smile. He smiled and waved back. "Night, Beth."

She bit her bottom lip, studying him. He waited, meeting her gaze. Finally she walked over to him, resolve in every step. She rested her hands on the arm of the chair and whispered, "I'm sorry your dad died."

"Thank you, Beth. I'm sorry your dad isn't here too. Maybe sometime you can tell me about your dad, and I'll tell you about mine."

She nodded, then ran across the room to the stairs.

"Thank you," Mandy said softly to him as the girls and Ellen reached the loft.

He turned to her in surprise. "For what?"

"For telling the girls about your loss. It's good for them to know there are adults who lost parents as children and survived. It's been awful for those girls since Zach left."

Jason's nails bit into the palms of his hands. "When I think of him abandoning those girls, I'd like to take him out behind a barn and teach him a lesson." He glanced at the pine-covered rafters and gave a short laugh. "No pun intended."

"Before Zach left I didn't know I was capable of almost hating someone. I keep asking God to help me forgive him."

Jason couldn't imagine sweet, patient Mandy hating anyone, even Zach. "I grieved when I lost my parents, but I knew they hadn't wanted to leave me. Beth and Bonnie know their father chose to leave them." He slammed his fist on the arm of the chair. "They're too young to experience that loss of trust."

"Yes, yet they're only two of millions of children experiencing it. All we can do is show them every day that there are still people in their lives who won't leave no matter how tough things get."

She was right, of course, but it didn't stop the girls' pain at the moment. Still, knowing the children had Mandy and Ellen in their lives calmed him somewhat. They'd never let the girls down.

Losing Mandy had hurt him almost more than losing his parents. He'd given her all his love, all his trust, and she'd chosen to leave him. On a much larger scale, that was the kind of rejection Beth and Bonnie must feel because of Zach's selfishness.

He forced his mind from the painful memory. "How did all of you end up living upstairs?"

Mandy curled deeper into the wing chair. "I turned your grandparents down when they first offered me the use of the barn. Ellen kept after me to rent it. I was living in Asheville.

Ellen and the girls lived here near Boone. After Zach left, Ellen didn't want to disrupt the girls' lives further by moving, but she needed someone close by for support." Mandy shrugged. "So I decided to rent the barn."

"And live in it."

"I only meant to live here until I found an apartment. Grandma Tillie and Grandpa Seth offered to let me stay with them, but. . ." Another shrug. This time her gaze wandered away from his. He knew it was because of him that she'd chosen not to stay with his grandparents.

She moved to the fireplace, opened the brass screen, and used a cast-iron poker to break a log into embers. "Things were tough for Ellen financially. Finally I realized it would be cheaper for all of us to live together here. Ellen and the girls loved the idea."

He walked to the hearth. Leaning his elbows against the massive oak beam mantel, he fingered a colorful wooden gnome sitting on a pine branch. "So now instead of just running a store, you help raise the girls."

She glanced at him sharply. "I like having the girls around. Ellen too."

"It wasn't an insult. It's like you to be generous with your home and time."

She poked especially hard at the log, and a chunk broke off with a sputter. "You make me sound like a saint."

"Hardly that. I remember a few faults." *Like not loving me enough to marry me.* His conscience immediately kicked in. That wasn't a fault, just the reality with which he'd had to learn to live.

"Only a few?" A teasing smile lit her eyes before she abandoned the topic. "Ellen and I expected to stay here for just a few months, but it's worked out well. In addition to helping me in the store, she's working as a bookkeeper for a clothing store, but it doesn't pay well. Living here gives her the time and money—barely—to take classes toward her accounting degree."

It probably never occurred to Mandy that most people don't consider themselves their sister's keeper, Jason thought. "Good for her. Sounds like she's got guts."

Mandy nodded, and he watched lights dance in her hair. "She has." She closed the grate and replaced the cast-iron poker in its stand. "So does Grandpa Seth. I'm sorry I missed visiting with him tonight. How is he doing?"

The weight of the world seemed to drop back onto his shoulders. "He's still scheduled for surgery first thing tomorrow."

She rested her hand on Jason's, but almost before his mind could register her hand's softness or his heart skip a beat at the joy from her once-familiar touch, she withdrew it. He pretended not to notice. Isn't that what she'd want? "Dr. Monroe says Gramps's chance of coming through well are good," he said, "but there's always a possibility. . ."

"The operation is so standard now. It's not as risky as it once was."

He nodded and wondered whether she could tell how forced his smile was. "Thanks for the reminder."

"You look so tired."

The huskiness in her voice drew his gaze to hers. The concern he saw there for himself warmed his heart. "I guess I am." He rested his forehead on the back of his hand. He'd thought himself strong enough to support his grandparents, but after only five days, weariness engulfed him. "When my parents died, Gram and Gramps were the strong ones, always there for me even though they'd lost a daughter. Now Gram leans on me. For the first time, I can see how vulnerable she is beneath the image she's worn all these years."

"Her strength has always rested in her faith in God, but I think the love between her and Grandpa Seth is another part of her strength."

He nodded. "And now she's afraid she might lose that." He sighed deeply and closed his eyes. "So am I."

"I'm so sorry this has happened, Jason."

Her soft voice and gentle touch on his arm brought sudden

tears to his eyes. He squeezed his lids tightly. He reached for her. Sliding his arms around her waist, he buried his face in her neck beneath a silky wave of hair to hide his tears from her. She stirred, and thinking she was going to pull away, he tightened his hold.

He felt her stiffen. Heard her gasp softly as if in surprise. Then she rested her palms on his shoulders. She barely touched him at first. Slowly she slipped her arms around his neck and hugged him tightly.

The strength he'd demanded of himself—forcing himself to stuff his emotions into hiding—collapsed. He felt it break, felt the emotions he'd struggled to dam up flood through him. With a shudder, a sob wrenched from him.

seven

Mandy felt Jason's chest jerk in his attempt to stifle a sob. The force of the buried cry seemed to rip through his body.

I love you, Jason. The words repeated in Mandy's mind while she held him. Her chest ached with her desire to heal the pain caused by the fear his grandfather might die, but she knew only God had that capability.

Besides, she had no reason to believe Jason wanted to hear her words of love. No reason to believe the words would give him even a modicum of comfort. No reason to believe he'd want the kiss she longed to press to his temple.

So she simply continued to hold him, her cheek against his hair, stroking the back of his head lightly, her heart crimped in empathy. Wonder at the familiarity of him filtered through her concern. Her hands and arms remembered the way he felt beneath her touch.

Soon his chest stopped heaving with the sobs he held within himself. His cheek remained on her shoulder where a warm dampness seeped through her sweater. She knew it was his tears. The knowledge brought tears to her own eyes.

They stood that way a long time. Finally his hold loosened, though his arms remained around her waist. He straightened, and Mandy loosened her hold also, resting her hands on his shoulders.

When his gaze met hers, she saw no tears in his eyes. Apprehension looked out from them, but he only said, "I'm sorry."

"You're entitled to worry about your grandfather."

"Yeah." He released his hold and stepped back. "I'd better get going. Need to get up early tomorrow. Gramps's surgery is scheduled for seven. Gram and I want to be there."

Mandy clasped her hands behind her back, trying to act as

though her heart wasn't slamming against her ribs from recently holding Jason in her arms. "I'll stop at the hospital too, if that's okay."

"Sure. Gram and Gramps would want you there."

But you don't? Mandy's heart asked the question she didn't dare voice.

Jason took a couple more steps back toward the door. "Want to ride to the hospital with us?"

"I'd better not. I may need to get back to the store before you're ready to return home."

"Then I'll see you at the hospital. Night."

"Good night." She spoke to his back as he hurried across the room. A moment later the bells above the door tinkled merrily as he left.

Mandy took a deep, shaky breath and lowered herself into the wing chair. She drew her legs up, wrapped her arms around her knees, closed her eyes, and allowed herself to relive the minutes holding Jason.

She'd spent years trying to forget how she'd felt in his arms, trying to forget how it felt to hold him.

"I haven't forgotten, Jason," she whispered, pain tightening her chest. "I haven't forgotten anything. And I've never stopped loving you, not for a moment."

❧

Jason slouched down, rested the back of his head against the top of the blue sofa, and let his gaze slowly scan the ivory-white waiting room walls. A picture of roses hung on each wall, adding color and impersonal cheer. A basket of pink-and-blue silk flowers—he didn't know what kind—rested amid stacks of magazines on the oval, oak coffee table in front of him. *A pity,* he thought, *that the flowers aren't real.* If they were, their fragrance might mask the hospital smells.

It had already been a long morning, and Gramps was still in surgery. Family of other patients had drifted in and out of the waiting room. Right now, Jason and Gram were alone. *No, not alone. God is here.*

The thought brought a bit of refreshment to Jason's spirit, though it didn't quiet all his fears. He silently repeated the petitions he'd made a number of times already: *Please, God, bring Gramps through this. Guide the surgical team. Give Gram and me strength.*

Jason wondered why Mandy hadn't shown up yet. It wasn't like her not to keep her word. Besides, she loved Gram and Gramps as much as her own kin.

The intensity with which he wanted her there surprised him. Beneath her vivacious energy lay a serenity and confidence in God's love which he longed for now.

Even so, embarrassment squirmed through his chest at the remembrance of the previous night. As an "enlightened male" he knew intellectually that it was okay for a man to cry, regardless of the messages a boy received growing up. But it didn't feel right. It was downright scary, his emotions getting away from him that way. Not that Mandy would think a man's tears a weakness.

The compassion he'd felt in her arms swept over him. He hadn't hung onto anyone during life's storms for a long time.

His glance slid to Gram, who sat beside him wearing a rose jogging suit. Was she wondering whether she and Gramps would ever hold each other again?

Rays of sunlight slipped through the window blinds behind them and laid pale yellow light on her gray hair. An open devotional book rested on top of the black leather-bound Bible in her lap. With the fingers of one hand, she played with the simple gold cross on the chain about her neck. Gramps had given her the cross on her sixtieth birthday, Jason remembered. She always wore it.

She looked small, sad, scared, and incredibly vulnerable—everything he wasn't accustomed to seeing in her spirit. Love and a desire to protect her rushed through him. He reached out, laid his arm across her shoulders, and gave her a squeeze.

She looked up, and his heart contracted at the fear he saw in her eyes.

"I keep asking God to bring Seth through this," she admitted. "I want to believe God will do just that. But I can't forget that we all die. That's the plan. Makes it hard to know what God's will is now."

He squeezed her shoulder again. "I have those same thoughts every time I pray."

She gave a little sigh and shifted until she leaned against him.

A movement caught Jason's attention. His spirits lifted at the sight of Mandy entering the waiting area at a quick pace. He shoved away the temptation to retreat behind a wall of embarrassment at his actions the night before and smiled a welcome.

Gram reached both hands toward Mandy. "You made it. I knew you would."

Jason felt the chill of the cold air Mandy brought with her from the outdoors as she grasped Gram's hands and kissed her cheek. "Sorry I couldn't get here sooner. The girl scheduled to work this morning called in sick. Ellen promised to drive for a class trip today, so she couldn't help out."

Gram continued to cling to Mandy's gloved hands. "You didn't close the store, did you?"

"No. A wife of one of your farm workers agreed to help out."

"That's good." Gram released Mandy's hands.

Mandy removed her gloves and gray winter jacket. Jason noticed that the cold wind had left her cheeks almost as bright as her red sweater.

She sat down near Gram on the edge of a blue club chair which stood at a right angle to the sofa. "Is Grandpa Seth still in surgery?"

Jason and Gram both nodded.

"Has anyone told you how it's going?" Mandy looked from Gram to Jason.

Jason shook his head. "No. We're hoping that's a good sign."

Mandy glanced at the round, oak-rimmed clock that hung above the small desk in one corner of the room. "Is it normal for the surgery to last this long?"

"According to Dr. Monroe, it is," he assured her. "It's a pretty complicated surgery. They strip arteries from his legs to replace the clogged arteries around his heart. Have to admit, though, I didn't know time could move this slow."

Gram leaned forward. "Which of the girls is on the class trip?"

Glad to think about anything other than the operation, Jason thought. *Can't blame her.*

"Bonnie. Her class is visiting a log cabin where women still spin wool and weave the old-fashioned way."

Gram's eyes brightened with interest. "The children will like that. My grandma had a loom. Grandpa built it for her when they were newlyweds. My, she made that shuttle fly. She wove beautiful rugs. Remind me to show you next time you're up to the house."

"I will." Mandy looked from Gram to Jason and back again. "Did Beth's teacher, Miss Lewis, get in touch with either of you? She wants the class to visit a Christmas tree farm."

"I thought the school didn't allow Christmas celebrations anymore," Gram said, "what with students from religions other than Christianity and that separation of church and school law."

"You're right, but the school does allow studies of different traditions. Beth's class is studying Christmas, Hanukkah, and Kwanza. Since Christmas trees are one of our state's largest businesses, no one should object to the class visiting a farm. Miss Lewis would like it to be yours, but Beth told her about Grandpa Seth's surgery, and Miss Lewis didn't want to impose on you."

"We'll be glad to have the class visit," Jason assured Mandy. "Right, Gram?"

Gram nodded. "We can give them a hayride. And hot apple cider and cookies afterward."

"I'll arrange the ride and a tour if you ladies take care of the eats," Jason agreed. It meant additional work at an already busy time, but it would be good public relations and give Gram something to look forward to. Besides, he wanted to do it. "It will be fun."

Mandy smiled at him. "I'll tell Miss Lewis to call you."

The conversation dried up. After a couple minutes, Mandy leaned forward and patted Gram's hand. "Are you doing all right?"

Gram gave her a thin smile. "As all right as a body can be at a time like this, I reckon. I'm trying to keep the faith, as they say, but. . .but it's his heart, you know?" Her voice faltered on the last words. "I mean, hearts are. . .vital."

Mandy patted Gram's hand again. "The doctors know what they're doing. There's no denying there's risk involved, but it's Grandpa Seth's best chance to stay here with us."

Gram nodded.

"I won't pretend I know how God's going to answer our prayers." Mandy's tone was gentle. "But remember what He said in Jeremiah: 'I know the plans I have for you, plans to prosper you and not to harm you, plans to give you a hope and a future.' He only has good in mind for Grandpa Seth and you and Jason."

Jason felt Gram's shoulders rise beneath his arm as she took a deep breath. "Thanks for reminding me," she said, her voice firmer than he'd heard all morning. "I'm glad you're here, Mandy. You're family, and our family didn't feel complete until you arrived."

"Thank you. This is exactly where I want to be right now."

Jason caught the glitter of tears in Mandy's eyes before she blinked them away.

It does feel right that Mandy's here, Jason thought. He didn't let himself explore the fact that she'd refused to formally join the family by marrying him. He hadn't enough emotional energy to deal with that now. *I'm just glad she's here, Lord. Thank You for bringing her back into my life.*

Mandy pulled two folded papers from her purse. "Beth and Bonnie made get-well cards for Grandpa Seth."

"How sweet." Gram accepted the papers.

Jason glanced down. Both homemade cards were addressed

to "Grandpa Seth." Jason smiled. It touched and amused him that the girls had adopted Mandy's name for his grandfather.

Beth's card showed a girl hugging a man with a beard. Beneath the picture she'd written in blue crayon, "This is me giving you a bear hug." Bonnie had drawn a girl sitting on a bearded man's lap and written in red, "I miss you. Come home soon."

Jason chuckled. "Gramps looks like Santa Claus in their pictures."

Mandy and Gram agreed, laughing.

Their conversation dwindled to a few comments and words of encouragement. They passed the Bible and devotional book back and forth among themselves until Dr. Monroe walked in with an infectious grin. "Seth held his own in there. The operation couldn't have gone better."

"Does that mean he'll be all right?" Hope filled Gram's face.

"There are no guarantees, but he has a great chance of recovering."

Gram's face relaxed somewhat. "Thank the Lord." She gave a mischievous grin. "And you, of course."

Dr. Monroe chuckled. "I don't mind not receiving top billing."

"Can we see him?" Gram's voice trembled.

"He's not awake yet. They're moving him back to ICU. He'll be there a couple days. Just standard procedure."

"When can we see him?" Gram asked.

"When he wakes up. Let me give you an idea of what to expect during the next couple months."

The next couple months. The words brought relief to Jason. They sounded so positive. Not the next couple hours or days—but months.

"Seth will be on a ventilator for a day and a half," Dr. Monroe continued. "That's normal, so don't let it worry you. Looks a little scary, but it's a good thing. After he wakes up, we'll get him out of bed and into a chair."

Jason started. "So soon?"

"He won't be staying there long, I assure you. A short while and then back to bed. After a couple days, if there are no complications, he'll be moved out of ICU. We'll keep him here four or five days longer, monitoring him until we're sure he's recovered sufficiently to go home."

Gram's grin widened. "Home."

Jason caught Mandy's glance and smiled. She smiled back, her eyes sparkling with the same joy he knew she saw in his eyes.

"I didn't think he'd be home before Thanksgiving," Gram admitted.

"Definitely by Thanksgiving, barring complications."

"Will he need medications?" Jason asked.

"Only aspirin. I don't want him doing anything too physically demanding for the first few weeks," the doctor warned.

"I suppose Seth needs to change his diet," Gram speculated dryly.

"Low fat, low cholesterol is the way to go. I'll talk with you about it in more detail before Seth is discharged. I've some brochures that might help you out." The doctor drew his pepper-and-salt eyebrows together. "Along with the physical issues, there are other important changes to watch for."

Unease slithered through Jason's chest. "What changes?"

"Depression is common after this kind of surgery. A lot of heart attack survivors become reflective, almost have a change in personality. They look back over their lives—see what they've done, what they wanted to do and didn't, what they may never have a chance to do now. Let me know if he gets depressed, but don't be surprised by it. It's normal. Seth's life has changed forever."

Jason nodded. *This has changed all of our lives forever.*

eight

Jason leaned against an old, white wooden pillar on his grandparents' back porch, removed his billed hat, and rubbed his red-plaid-flannel-covered forearm across his forehead. He glanced at his watch. Only time for a quick break before Beth's class arrived.

He breathed the crisp mountain air in deeply, relishing the pleasure of spending a day outdoors in the mountains instead of inside his Wall Street office. Looking at his hat, he grinned. ASU for his alma mater—Appalachian State University—stood proudly in gold against the black background. The cap was worn, the colors faded. Gram had found it in the attic yesterday.

The hat brought back memories—some fun, some fond, some not so pleasant. Fun memories of the companionship he'd found as part of the college baseball team. Fond memories of meeting Mandy and the relationship that grew quickly to love. Not-so-pleasant memories of Mandy refusing to marry him.

He wrenched his thoughts from the past and forced them to the scene before him. Mountain ridges spread into the distance like stilled waves. They were covered with Christmas trees, which looked like green pyramids standing in orderly rows. The scene, as always, filled him with awe and quiet joy. In spite of the fourteen- to sixteen-hour days he and the other men put in, he loved this work and this place. If it weren't for Gramps's heart condition and Jason's knowledge that Neal and the other partners back in New York were overworked because of his absence, Jason would have felt completely content.

"Mandy's presence would still have played havoc with that contentment," he admitted with a wry shake of his head to a scarlet cardinal in a nearby holly bush.

Moving color in the form of people and trucks filled the Christmas groves: men cutting trees, carrying trees, stuffing trees into binders and pulling them out, piling the trees on trucks. Besides Ted, who'd helped Gramps manage the farm, eight men worked on the farm year-round. That number neared thirty with the locals and college students hired this time of year.

Business was going well. All the overseas orders had been shipped, as well as orders to retailers in distant states, along with most of the live trees, which were shipped with ball and burlap around their roots. This coming week—the week before Thanksgiving—would be a challenge. Gramps had retail lots in Atlanta, Charlotte, Winston-Salem, Raleigh, and other large cities. It took two truckloads of trees a day just to keep the lots in Atlanta stocked. No rest for the weary here.

He stretched his arms over his head and winced. He thought he'd have worked out all the creaks and crimps in his joints and muscles by now.

"Hi, Jason."

"Hey, Mandy." He lowered his arms as she stopped at the bottom of the steps. She looked great in a red-and-black-checked wool coat. She looked good in anything, for that matter, but he especially liked to see her in bright, cheerful colors. "What are you doing out of the store? It's only one o'clock; a lot of hours left before quitting time."

"Beth's teacher asked if I'd act as a chaperon for the tour this afternoon. The school requires one adult for every seven children on field trips. One of the class mothers who'd pledged her time for today called in sick. You won't mind if I tag along, will you?"

"The more the merrier." He glanced at his watch again. "The kids should arrive anytime now."

"They're already here. Grandma Tillie was leaving the store when they arrived. She asked me to find you."

He took the four wooden stairs in two steps. "I'd better get a move on."

"It's okay." Mandy fell into step beside him. "She's taken the class to the nursery. She said she'd start the tour there, and you can take over when you catch up with the group."

"I'm surprised she left Gramps alone."

"He's napping, so she took advantage of the time to bring her frosted sugar cookies down to the store. That's where we'll serve the kids cider and cookies after your tour and the hayride. I don't think she'd leave him for a moment except for the cell phones you bought them." Mandy gave a bright laugh. "She keeps her phone in a carrier attached to her belt. She said she feels like a cowboy wearing a six-shooter."

He chuckled.

"It was a great idea you had," Mandy continued, "that Grandpa Seth, Grandma Tillie, you, and I carry phones with us and then programming all our numbers in so Grandma Tillie or Grandpa Seth can reach any of us in an emergency with just the touch of a button."

"The phones are worth the cost in peace of mind."

"Here's my phone." Mandy held it up. "I've decided to get a holder like Grandma Tillie's. That way there'll be no chance I'll set the phone down and forget it someplace."

"Your dedication to them means a lot to me."

"They're special people. I've loved them since we first met."

He remembered that meeting. He'd introduced them, confident he'd found the girl of his dreams, confident she'd one day be part of their family.

Mandy stuck her phone in her pocket. "Grandpa Seth is certainly glad to be home."

"That he is. In the two days he's been back, he's given Gram more than her share of headaches. I don't remember Gramps showing much temper down through the years, but he sure is ornery now. Doesn't like being dependent on Gram, I suppose." Jason reached to open the door to the nursery. "Guess I wouldn't like depending on someone else either."

Mandy's eyes flashed with teasing laughter as she moved past him. "Ah, yes, you independent mountain men."

Her friendly, fun manner bordered on flirtatious. Jason caught himself just in time from kissing the lips smiling up at him. The realization jolted him and roughened his voice when he replied, "You mountain women hold your own with us."

"We do our best."

Mandy's response was almost lost in Gram's greeting. "You're just in time, Jason. I've told the children all about how Christmas trees start as tiny seeds in the crevices of pine cones, then are grown in here until they're strong enough to survive outside. I'll let you tell them about the rest of the Christmas tree business."

"Thank you, Gram." He raised one hand high in greeting. "Welcome to the Always Christmas Farm."

As he smiled at the children returning his greeting, he thought, *Those third-grade mountain boys have no idea what's in store for them in a few years from those future sixth-grade mountain girls.*

❧

Mandy stood, hands in her jacket pockets, behind the children at the edge of a grove of Fraser firs.

"It smells like Christmas out here," one little girl said.

The adults laughed, but the other children chimed in to agree with their classmate.

"It always smells like Christmas here," Beth said. Her dry tone spoke volumes of the sense of ownership she felt for the farm that had in such an unexpected manner become her home. Beth stood right in front of Jason. *As if claiming ownership of him too,* Mandy thought. She wished Beth dared let her guard down and allow herself to like Jason, but she realized that might make it more difficult for Beth when Jason returned to New York.

Mandy looked over the children to where Jason stood. It felt luxurious, this opportunity to openly watch Jason without worrying he or anyone else would think her indiscreet.

His looks hadn't changed much in the eight years since they'd stopped seeing each other. He was still trim, and his hair hadn't started graying, but his skin had lost the fresh look of youth and gained a tougher texture. The laugh lines at the corner of his eyes had deepened and now stayed visible whatever his expression.

The largest difference was the sense of maturity. Anyone meeting him would immediately recognize him as a man who carried responsibilities well. She felt a twinge in her chest. He'd grown into a fine man. Any woman would be honored to be loved by such a man. And she'd turned his love down. She'd make the same decision today given the same circumstances. But there was a difference—today she'd make that decision knowing she'd never stop missing him.

"There are many kinds of Christmas trees," Jason was saying. "The trees in this grove are Fraser firs. Some people call Frasers the Cadillac of Christmas trees. Frasers have strong branches with short needles, so it's easy to hang ornaments on them. Come close and look at the needles on these trees." The group shifted closer to the trees on either side of him. Some of the children reached out to feel the needles. "As we go through the farm, I'll show you how to tell the different kinds of Christmas trees apart. Notice that the needles on these Fraser firs are flat, a rich, dark green on top, and silvery underneath."

His words opened a memory in Mandy's heart. The night they met, they'd gone with a group of friends to a pizza parlor. Long after the others went home, Jason and Mandy had stayed, talking into the night, learning pieces of each other's lives and hearts. He'd looked across the table, playing with the straw in his empty soda glass, and said, "Your eyes are the same shade of green as Fraser fir needles in the sunlight."

She'd laughed, truly amused to hear her eyes compared to the needles of a tree, but secretly she'd felt a deep joy at his comment. Already she'd learned how he loved trees, especially the royal Fraser fir.

Two tractors pulling large, hay-filled wagons chugged to a stop nearby, jolting her back to the Christmas farm. At Jason's command, the group climbed into the wagons and selected places to sit in the scratchy, sweet-smelling hay.

The children sang Christmas songs as tractors pulled the wagons between groves of different kinds of trees. At each stop Jason explained more about the trees and business. He described the care that went into a tree for the seven to ten years it took for a tree to grow from a seedling to a treasured part of someone's Christmas: keeping weeds and grass mowed, fertilizing the trees, shearing them to keep the near-perfect triangular shape people like. "We spray the trees for pests too. That's important. The wrong pests can wipe out an entire crop of trees."

He invited the children to gently touch the trees, study the shape and feel of the needles, and smell the trees. "Not all Christmas trees smell the same. Rub the needles of this Douglas fir. They smell a bit lemony, don't you think?"

Mandy watched Jason introduce the children to the trees, watched the excitement that radiated from him, the tenderness in the way his large fingers touched the needles. A strange combination of quiet joy and sadness filled her. He seemed made for this world. The man who'd burst into her store the day after Grandpa Seth's heart attack, the man whose picture accompanied articles in business magazines wasn't the Jason Garth she knew. In spite of the years he'd worked in New York, she couldn't imagine this man in the billed black-and-gold college cap and tan corduroy jacket living the life of a high-powered executive in one of the world's most powerful cities.

The children's delighted laughter broke into her thoughts. Jason had spread the branches of a fir to reveal a bird's nest. He led the children to a nearby tree and showed them where a deer had nibbled at the tender growth. At another spot he pointed out where he'd found a wild turkey nest. For the rest of the ride, the children kept a lookout for wildlife, not even disappointed that they saw only small birds, squirrels, and one rabbit.

A boy with thick brown hair that reached his eyebrows shifted to his knees in the crackling hay. "I bet there's bears around here too, aren't there, Mr. J. P.? And wolves and panthers."

The relish with which the boy envisioned dangerous wild creatures running free on the farm amused Mandy.

Beth groaned. "You're just trying to scare us girls, Andy. There's no dangerous animals around here, are there, J. P.?"

Mandy saw Jason's hesitation and knew he was searching for an honest answer that wouldn't frighten the children. "It's true there are dangerous animals in the mountains, Beth, but they seldom stray out of the deep forests into civilized areas like this."

Beth and Andy exchanged I-told-you-so looks.

When the wagons returned to the nursery, Jason led the children into the one-story, warehouse-looking building where workers boxed trees to send to individuals and made wreaths and roping at long tables.

"You send Christmas trees in the mail?" A red-haired, freckled, skinny boy looked skeptical.

"Yes. We ship trees to some faraway places: Canada, the Virgin Islands, Chicago, Phoenix, Hawaii, Miami—"

"My grandparents live in Miami," the boy interrupted. "Did you send a tree to them?"

Mandy grinned as she watched Jason struggle to keep from laughing.

"I'm not sure. I don't personally address all the packages we ship out. Maybe you should write your grandparents and ask them."

The boy nodded, his expression sober. "I'm going to e-mail them and tell them they should buy one from you 'cause you have the best trees."

"We sent my grandparents a Christmas tree from here," Beth announced. "They live in Texas."

"That's right," Mandy agreed. "And now it's time for us to head to the Christmas store for cookies and hot apple cider.

The children cheered and headed for the door.

"Do you have time to join us for a snack?" Mandy asked Jason.

He hesitated. "I should get back to work."

"Will your conscience allow you to stay a few minutes if you tell it hot cider will warm you up and give you extra energy?"

Jason grinned. "Hot cider does sound good. Okay to invite the guys who drove the tractors?"

"Absolutely."

When Mandy and Jason entered the store, the children were following Beth and Miss Lewis to the local crafters' display room at the back. The group moved slowly, the boys' and girls' eyes wide as they viewed the trees, the limbs heavy with ornaments. Heads tilted back, necks stretched, the children looked at the pine roping, strings of plastic cranberries and popcorn, dolls, gnomes, and wooden cars that hung from the rafters.

"Wow!"

"Look at that—a Christmas tree covered in teddy bears."

"I never saw one of those before."

"I never saw so many Christmas trees at one time before."

"Yes, you did. We just saw thousands of Christmas trees outside."

"Not decorated ones."

"Santa's workshop must look like this."

"There is no Santa Claus."

"Is so. You just think there isn't because you're such a bully that Santa doesn't bring you anything for Christmas."

"Does so. Hey, look at the train beneath that tree. Boy, I'd sure like one of those."

Mandy and Jason shared laughing glances, and in doing so almost bumped into three girls exclaiming in rapturous terms over three child-sized angels dressed in ivory silk overlaid with gold-starred gauze. The couple carefully worked their way past the girls to follow another girl who danced down the narrow aisle between trees, singing along with the Charlotte Church rendition of "Mary's Boy Child" which played over the store's sound system.

Andy pushed past his singing classmate and stopped short in front of Jason and Mandy. "Mr. J. P., why aren't there any real Christmas trees in here? These are all fake."

Mandy swallowed a groan. Artificial Christmas trees weren't popular with Christmas tree farmers. She'd heard all the they-aren't-good-for-business-and-our-local-economy arguments.

Jason folded his arms across his chest and smiled an overly sweet smile at her. "Maybe we should ask Miss Wells since she's the store's owner."

Andy turned to Mandy. "How come?"

Mandy smiled back at Jason, thinking, *I can smile sweet too, Mister.* "Real trees would die, so we'd need to replace them every few weeks. That would make a lot of work and take a lot of time. Real trees might also cause a fire hazard. We use lights on every tree and leave the lights turned on much longer than most people do on their Christmas trees at home."

"Oh." Andy considered her explanation for a minute. "I see. But I still like real trees better."

"So do I," Mandy agreed.

The boy turned away, his attention caught by a large wooden truck beneath the artificial fir standing beside them.

"I guess it does seem strange to have a store filled with artificial trees on a Christmas tree farm," Mandy admitted as she and Jason continued walking.

"You don't sell the trees, do you? Just decorations?"

Incredulous, she stared at him. "Of course we don't sell these trees. Do you think we'd compete with Grandpa Seth's business?"

His lips twitched, and she realized he'd been teasing.

"We don't sell wreaths or roping either," she informed him. As they passed a tree covered with colorful old-fashioned ornaments from Germany, she added, "Did you notice the wreaths on the door and behind the counter are real?"

"Yes. And Gram says you'll be displaying our wreaths outside near the front door, where tourists who aren't in a position to buy a tree from us might be tempted to purchase a wreath they can easily carry in their cars. Thanks."

Mandy noted a bit of a grudging tone to his words but chose

to ignore it. "Two live trees with their roots bundled standing on either side of the door might be nice too. We could decorate them with red ribbons, carved birds, and real pine cones."

"Great idea. I'll tell one of the men to bring them down. I suppose you're expecting a rush over the Thanksgiving weekend?"

"Yes." Now that she'd started thinking about using real trees, ideas sprouted. "I suppose it wouldn't be too terribly dangerous to have one live tree inside. Maybe next to the door, where the visitors will catch the fragrance when they enter. I could use the coolest lights available on it and not keep them on all day and evening. Of course, I'd need to remember to check the water every day."

When he didn't respond, she glanced up at him.

He looked straight ahead, his expression sober. "You don't need to do that, Mandy. I know real trees in a place like this are a fire hazard, just like you said. Even Christmas tree farmers like me know that."

"I know you do. But it might be nice, just one real tree. I'll think about it." Then it struck her. He'd said, "Even Christmas tree farmers like me." Did he realize he'd identified himself as a tree farmer, not just a financial expert substituting for a tree farmer? She chose not to comment on it. Likely he'd only become defensive, say it was a slip of the tongue. She happened to believe there were no slips in the words people spoke, but a logical Wall Street man wasn't apt to agree.

At the entrance to the local crafters' room, Mandy smiled at Miss Lewis, who returned the smile with a shake of her head. "The children love your store, Mandy."

"Maybe while the kids eat, Jason can give them some safety tips for their Christmas trees at home."

"That's a great idea," Miss Lewis agreed. "I'll round up the children and get them settled while you get ready, Mandy."

"Ready for what?" Jason's brows met in a curious glance at Mandy.

Mandy darted him a mischievous grin. "You'll see."

nine

Jason looked at the group of whispering and giggling children seated on the wide, wooden floor planks and marveled at Miss Lewis's ability to so quickly draw the children from the Christmas wonders in the larger room and bring order to the group. Now they sat while Miss Lewis and the chaperons passed out frosted sugar cookies and Styrofoam cups filled with fragrant, warm apple cider.

Of course, Christmas items for children and the adult chaperons to drool over filled this room too. His gaze wandered the wooden walls. A quilt hanging held a place of honor, dark green squares framing a picture of Mary, Joseph, and baby Jesus beneath a lean-to style manger. Quilted and embroidered stockings hung from the deep window ledge. A tree covered with patchwork ornaments, straw figures, and popcorn strings stood on one side of the window. On the other, white crocheted snowflakes, stars, and angels danced on tree limbs.

Carved wooden toys—some painted, some not—sat about the room. Rag dolls and dolls with china faces and homemade dresses silently tempted little girls and mothers and grandmothers. Tin candle holders and cookie cutters sparkled from the top of a twig table. Pottery dishes and ornaments sat on a log table. Jason wondered whether Tom Berry had made that pottery. Handmade baskets—some woven of pine needles, some of oak—hung from the rafters. Other baskets filled with ornaments were scattered about the room.

A cane-seated oak rocking chair with a fir-green throw tossed over the back sat invitingly near the window, where handblown glass ornaments captured the sunlight. On the floor beside the chair, a baby doll in a hand-embroidered white gown lay in a small wooden cradle.

When all the children had received their cookies and drinks, Jason gave them pointers on how to care for their Christmas trees to reduce the chances of fire. He headed to the back of the room when he finished.

Mandy's sister, Ellen, handed him a cup of cider.

"Thanks. Where did you come from?"

"I just got home from my classes. What do you think of this room? It's Mandy's pride and joy."

"She told me it's the local crafters' room. Does that mean everything in here is made by local people?"

"Yes."

"I had no idea this area held so much talent." Jason's gaze swept the room again, this time with a new sense of respect. As a businessperson, he realized what it meant to devote an entire room to local work. But maybe it was a wise move. The room certainly embodied a homey, family-Christmas atmosphere.

Ellen nudged him with her elbow. "Here comes Mandy. Did I make it back in time for her show?"

"Uh, yes, I think so." Jason's curiosity stirred again. What was this show?

Mandy's dress only increased his curiosity. A huge old-fashioned bib apron of rough, off-white material covered her clothes. The apron touched the tops of her shoes and completely hid her slacks. She'd wrapped a white knit shawl over her shoulders.

Jason shifted his weight from one foot to the other as Mandy stopped in front of the window. He should get back to work. The men who drove the tractors had already finished their cider and headed out to the trees. Maybe he'd just stay a couple minutes and see what Mandy was up to.

Miss Lewis introduced Mandy's program. "Miss Wells prepared a special surprise. She's going to tell you a Christmas story from long ago. The story took place in a section of the Appalachians farther north than these mountains. In 1752, before the American Revolution and before the United States became a country, the French and some Native American tribes were battling with the British and other North American tribes over who would control America. Two hundred years later, Paul Gallico wrote this story down. He called it 'Miracle in the Wilderness.' " She brought her index finger to her lips in the universal "quiet" sign. "Listen while Miss Wells tells us what happened on Christmas all those years ago."

Jason noticed the ever-present music had changed to Christmas hymns played on a harpsichord. No words conflicted with the story. The instrumental music seemed appropriate for a story from the 1700s.

Mandy drew her shawl close about her shoulders and shivered visibly. "It was cold on Christmas Eve in 1752 as Jasper Adams and his wife Dorcas stumbled through the snow-covered forest with their Algonquian captors." She knelt and lifted the baby doll from the small wooden cradle beside the rocking chair. "Colder than the air was the fear in Jasper's and Dorcas's hearts for their eight-month-old son, whom one of the Algonquian carried on his shoulder."

Mandy explained how the little family had become captured. So skillful was Mandy's telling of the tale, she drew Jason completely into the story until he felt the cold and the fear and later the wonder. When the first miracle was revealed, it seemed to Jason that he could see the buck, doe, and fawn kneeling in the midst of the forest in honor of Christ's birth. Jason felt the courage it took for Jasper Adams to tell, at the fierce Algonquian leader's insistence, of the Child who caused the animals to pay Him homage. He felt the Algonquian leader's awe at the miracle in the wilderness, his respect for Jasper's God—the respect that caused him to release Jasper and his family in a second miracle.

Jason was so enraptured by the story that when it ended, he discovered his cider had grown cold. He'd planned to stay only a few minutes before returning to work. Half an hour had passed during the storytelling.

For a full minute after the story ended, the children sat transfixed, leaning forward, their gazes riveted on Mandy.

Then the children gave a common sigh and sat back.

Customers who'd wandered close enough to hear Mandy's voice had stayed to hear the entire story. Now they too stirred and drifted back to their shopping, murmuring to each other, "Wasn't that a beautiful story?" and "Lovely, just lovely."

Beside him, Ellen took a deep breath. "Guess I'd best get out front and help with the customers."

Jason lifted his shoulders in a stretch. Time for him to go too. A question stopped him.

Andy raised his hand. "Miss Wells, is that story true?"

"I don't know. The author wrote that his great-grandmother told him the story."

"I like the story, even if it's not true," Beth asserted.

A chorus of agreements rose from the class.

Jason smiled, amused and touched by Beth's attempt to protect Mandy's reputation with her fellow students.

"But deer don't know about Jesus," Andy persisted.

How is she going to field that? Jason wondered. He didn't envy her this predicament.

"I guess," Mandy started slowly. "I don't know what deer do and don't know. But I believe in miracles."

Miss Lewis stood. "Thank you for the story, Miss Wells. Class, put on your coats. It's time to go back to school."

Jason frowned slightly. Was she wondering if inadvertently she'd allowed Mandy to creep over the boundary between church and state? He didn't believe the story crossed that well-watched line, but another might interpret it differently.

"Do I have to go back to school too, Miss Lewis?" Beth asked.

"No, you can stay here since the school day is almost over."

"Yeah!" Beth skipped over to Mandy. "I liked that story."

Andy turned back to Mandy while zipping up his red jacket. "I'm part Cherokee." A challenge underlaid his tone.

Jason tensed, watching for Mandy's reaction. Amazing that the simple story brought up so many issues.

"That's a fine heritage." Mandy smiled at Andy. "Your people lived in these mountains a long time before America became the United States."

"The Cherokee were like the Algonquian in your story. They didn't believe Jesus is the Son of God. I don't either, but I like your story anyway." Andy spun about and pushed past a red-haired boy, apparently eager to leave before Mandy could reply.

Jason nodded to the students as they passed him on their way out. Most thanked him for the tour. Their enjoyment of the day left a smile in his heart.

Over the last of the students' thanks, Jason heard Beth's troubled question to Mandy.

"God punishes people who don't believe in Jesus, doesn't He?"

Jason glanced over at the girl. Mandy slipped her arms about Beth's shoulders and dropped a kiss on the top of the girl's head. "God is love, and I think God loves your classmate, don't you?"

Beth nodded, still frowning.

"Since God is love, I think we can trust Him to do what's best for people whether or not they believe in Jesus."

"I guess so." Beth didn't look convinced.

"There are some cookies left. Will you do me a favor and take the plate around to customers and offer them cookies?"

Beth brightened immediately at the prospect of such an important duty. She lifted the green-and-blue pottery plate from the table near the entrance, gave Jason a blinding smile, and moved into the large room, stepping slowly so as not to drop the plate.

Jason walked over to Mandy. "When did you become such a great storyteller?"

She furrowed her brow as if puzzled, but her eyes sparkled with fun. "Is that a compliment or a question?"

"Both."

"Then I thank you for the compliment, kind sir. As for the question, anyone can tell stories."

"Not everyone stirs their audience's emotions the way you did today."

She looked down and played with the shawl's fringe. "It was the story that touched people, not me."

"It was both." *So like her to be humble about her talent,* he thought. "Andy sure came up with some challenging questions. Beth too."

"Whew. I'll say."

He started the oak chair rocking with a push from his foot. "So you don't believe God punishes people?"

"I didn't say that. I said I believe He loves people. I believe we can trust that love to do what's best for every person." She slipped off the shawl and began folding it. "Besides, I'm concerned about Beth. I think she's angry with God. If that's true, she's likely also worried He will punish her for that anger. I believe trusting in His love for her will help her get over her anger faster than worrying He might punish her."

"She's only—eight? Why would she be angry at God?"

"Because—"

"Oh, of course," he interrupted. "Because her dad left."

Mandy nodded. "She's really hurting." She glanced past his shoulder. "Here she comes." She lifted her voice. "The plate's empty. The customers must have liked the cookies. Thanks for doing that, Honey."

"You're welcome. Mom says can you please help with the customers 'cause it's busy."

"Sure." Mandy dropped the shawl on the chair and reached behind her back to untie the enveloping apron. "Will you take the plate up to the loft kitchen, Beth? Thanks." She slipped the apron off, grabbed the shawl, and started to the outer room.

"Bye," Jason called out.

She looked back over her shoulder and smiled, continuing her hurried steps. "Bye. Thanks for all you did for Beth's class today."

"Yes, thanks, J. P." Beth smiled. "It was fun riding through the trees in the wagon."

"Glad you enjoyed it. I'd better get back to work before I'm fired."

She giggled, walking alongside him, carrying the plate. "Grandpa Seth wouldn't fire you."

"Don't think so?" He gave a strand of her blond hair a playful yank. "If he gives me a hard time, I'll send you to stand up for me. How's that?"

"All right." Her giggles continued as she headed for the loft.

Once outside, Jason's steps quickened into a jog. His thoughts stayed back at the Christmas barn while he ran. Was Mandy right, was Beth angry at God as well as Zach? Jason hated to think of all the hurt that sweet kid carried inside her because of her selfish father.

Zach has a lot to answer for.

ten

Mandy hummed along to Bing Crosby's "White Christmas" while gently tucking a handblown purple-and-gold tree topper surrounded in bubble wrap into a box. A steady stream of customers had filled the store all day. Even now at two-fifty-something, women in the middle of the room were trying to decide on which buildings to add to their Snow Village collections. Mandy was accustomed to taking advantage of "spare" minutes such as this to work on small tasks like this mailing. Beside her, Ellen stuck price tags on pieces of pottery dinnerware Tom Berry had just brought in.

We're a good team. The thought added pleasure to Mandy's already-happy day. She felt blessed, doing work she loved with someone she loved.

Mandy scooped Styrofoam beads up with an old plastic measuring cup from the large plastic bag stored behind the counter and filled the remaining space in the cardboard box.

"Did you notice how he watched you yesterday?" Ellen studied the Christmas design on one of the plates, but her attention was obviously elsewhere.

"Who watched me?" Mandy's brows met in puzzlement. "What are you talking about?"

"J. P. He watched you while you told that story."

"Everyone in the room watched me. I was the only person talking."

Ellen set the plate down on the counter. "I mean he really watched you, the way a man watches a woman he really likes."

Mandy's heart rate picked up speed at Ellen's words, but she shook her head. "You saw what you wanted to see. Jason isn't interested in me that way. Not anymore." *Not that I'd mind if he were.*

"You're not going to try to convince me there's still been no kisses between you?"

Mandy reached for the wide roll of postal tape. "Definitely no kisses."

"Right." Ellen's dry tone clearly announced that she didn't believe such nonsense.

The two customers approached the counter with their Snow Village purchases, preventing further discussion even if Ellen had been inclined to force the issue. While Mandy rang up the orders and Ellen bagged the purchases, the customers chatted happily about their Snow Village collections.

Beth, Bonnie, and Tom Berry came out from the local crafters' room as the customers left. The girls were only half-way between the back room and the front counter when Jason entered carrying a stack of plastic food containers.

"Hi, J. P." Beth and Bonnie raced toward him, each flinging their arms around him when they reached him. "I got here first," Bonnie announced.

Beth lifted her chin. "Who cares?" Her haughty tone made it clear she cared.

Jason grinned. "Whoa. A professional football team could use you two."

Watching the girls giggling at his teasing, Mandy felt her heart soften. Jason seemed so at ease with the girls. He and Tom were good for Beth and Bonnie. Perhaps the girls didn't find the men threatening since neither of them were in the position of a father figure.

Chuckling, Jason freed himself from the girls and set the plastic cartons down on the counter between Mandy and Ellen. "I come bearing gifts. Gram is afraid you two are working too hard and not eating properly, so she sent dinner. Grilled chicken and steamed vegetables." He nodded at Tom. "Hi."

"Mmm." Mandy opened the chicken container, leaned down to smell, and closed her eyes. "Wonderful."

Ellen grabbed the container. "Hey, share it. I'm starved."

Tom grinned and closed the cover. "Plates and silverware

might be a good idea."

Ellen waved her hand. "What, you've never heard of picnics and finger foods?"

"Fingers might work for the chicken, but for steamed veggies?" Tom shook his head. "You'd end up with mushed vegetables."

His description set the girls on another giggling spree.

Ellen heaved an exaggerated sigh. "Okay, if you insist, we'll use plates and silverware. Beth, would you run upstairs and get some dishes for us?"

"Okay." She skipped between glittering trees to the loft staircase.

Ellen picked up one of the pottery plates she'd priced earlier. "This dinnerware you made is almost too beautiful to eat off, Tom."

"I suppose that's a compliment, but I hope your customers don't feel it's too pretty to use. I'll sell a lot more if they buy it to put on their tables than if they buy an odd piece to display."

Bonnie climbed up onto a stool. Beside her, Jason leaned against the counter. "I had the trees you wanted for beside the front door brought down about an hour ago, Mandy."

Mandy straightened. "Thanks. Now I can decorate them in time for the Thanksgiving weekend shopping rush. Will you help me decorate them, Bonnie?"

"Sure."

"I've decided to use a real tree inside too," Mandy told Jason. "I think it will be perfect for the Mitten Tree."

Jason's brow furrowed. "Mitten Tree?"

"Pastor talked about it in church Sunday. Don't you remember?" Bonnie reproached.

" 'Fraid not. Suppose you tell me about it."

"Well." Bonnie took a deep breath. "People bring mittens and hang them on the mitten tree, and Mandy gives them a free Christmas tree ornament."

Jason nodded. "I see. And why does Mandy want a tree full of mittens?"

"They aren't for her." Bonnie cast her gaze at the ceiling. "They're Christmas presents for kids whose parents can't afford to buy them mittens."

"Sounds like a great idea."

Mandy thanked him with a smile.

"If you pick out a tree, I'll see it's brought down here and set up," he told her. "Consider it the Garth donation to the mitten cause."

"Thank you."

"Planning to take time off from the Christmas tree business to celebrate Thanksgiving, J. P.?" Tom asked.

"Part of the day. After Gramps's heart attack, I'd hate to completely miss spending the holiday with them. We're trying to get all our retail lots set up before the Thanksgiving weekend rush begins, and that usually means our people work Thanksgiving. Hate to take the whole day off when our people can't do the same."

Tom nodded. "I see your point, but if you can spare half an hour or so, I'd like your help. I have a large nativity to set up. An outdoor one. The pieces are pretty heavy."

"I'll work it in. Speaking of work, I'd better get back to it."

"Aren't you going to eat with us?" Bonnie asked.

"I ate with Gram and Gramps."

From beside the cash register, Mandy picked up an envelope from the pile of mail that had arrived that day. It was the first chance she'd had to open it. "Thanks for bringing us the leftovers, Jason. And the trees."

Jason waved and started toward the door.

As Mandy slit the envelope with a silver letter opener, the phone rang.

"I'll get it." Bonnie grabbed for the phone. "Always Christmas Shop. This is Bonnie. How can I help you?"

Mandy listened to Bonnie's prim phone voice with half her attention, the other half on her mail. She and Ellen preferred the girls not answer the store phone, but knowing it was inevitable the girls would sometimes do so, they had taught them to answer in a professional manner.

"Daddy!"

Bonnie's squeal of delight caused Mandy's stomach to turn over in a nauseous sense of foreboding. Out of the corner of her eye, she saw Jason stop and turn around just inside the door.

Her glance darted to Ellen. Her eyes filled with apprehension, Ellen watched her happy daughter.

Tom's gaze also rested on Ellen, his lips pressed tightly together.

Bonnie continued her conversation, blissfully unaware of the tension with which her father's call had flooded the usually cheery store. "I miss you, Daddy. Where are you? What are you doing?" The child's eyes were large with excitement.

None of the adults spoke.

Beth's quick footsteps sounded as she descended the stairs and came across the room, carrying a stack of plates, forks, and knives. Tom took them from her and set them on the counter.

Bonnie held out the phone to Beth. "Here."

Beth reached for the receiver. "Who is it?"

"Daddy."

Surprise and joy filled Beth's eyes. Then red color surged across her face. Her eyes shuttered. She handed the receiver back. "I don't want to talk to him." She turned and ran back across the room toward the stairs.

eleven

For a moment the only sound in the room was Beth's retreating footsteps thudding against the wooden floor and stairs. Mandy, her heart crimped in pain for the girl, stared after her.

"Give me that." Ellen grabbed the phone, breaking the illusion of a frozen setting. She turned her back to Bonnie in what Mandy guessed was an attempt to hide her anger. But Mandy saw the fury flash in her sister's eyes, and Ellen's voice held little restraint when she spoke. "Why are you calling, Zach?"

Jason moved quickly to Bonnie and slipped an arm around her shoulders. "Why don't you come outside with me and check out the trees I brought for your aunt Mandy? See if you think they're all right or if we need to select some other ones."

"Okay." Bonnie slid off the stool, her gaze still on her mother.

Mandy mouthed a silent "thank you" to Jason, warmth filling her chest at his desire to spare Bonnie from witnessing anger between her parents. Especially when the gesture took him away from his work.

Mandy started around the counter. She wanted to get out of earshot of Ellen and Zach's conversation too. Should she go with Jason and Bonnie or go after Beth? She wavered a moment. Would Beth want someone to talk with right away, or did she need some time alone? Rather than barging in, maybe it would be wiser to let Ellen talk with Beth.

Mandy's decision made, she addressed Bonnie brightly. "Is it all right if I come too? I haven't seen the trees yet either."

"Sure, the more the merrier." Jason's voice was more jovial than the simple event normally justified. "What do you say, Bonnie?"

"Yeah, sure."

Mandy doubted Bonnie realized what she was agreeing to. Though she followed Jason, she looked over her shoulder, her troubled gaze on Ellen.

Tom followed them out the door. "Think someone should check on Beth?" he whispered in Mandy's ear.

His concern for Beth increased Mandy's admiration of him. "Let's give Beth a few minutes alone. If she doesn't come downstairs soon, I'm sure Ellen will check on her."

Brass carriage lamps on either side of the door lit the entrance area, in addition to the lighted icicles which decorated the roof. Together they supplied enough light to see the Fraser firs in their burlap bags.

Jason engaged Bonnie in a serious consideration of the trees. Did she like the kind he'd chosen? The height? The shape? Did she think they matched each other well?

Bonnie took time to think through each question before answering, walking around the trees, standing back to view them. In the end, she complimented Jason. "These are perfect."

Mandy stood near the heavy wooden red door, rubbing her sweatered arms and shivering, wishing she'd grabbed a coat. "Will you help me decorate the trees, Bonnie? I thought I'd use red ribbons and wooden birds."

"The little painted birds?" Bonnie's face brightened. "The cardinals and blue jays?"

"Those are the ones."

"Oh, they'll be just right. Let's get them now."

Mandy hesitated, not ready to go back within hearing distance of Ellen and Zach's conversation.

Bells jangled as the door opened. Sweet strains of "O, Little Town of Bethlehem" with its message of peace floated onto the night air as Ellen stepped outside.

Everyone looked at her, but no one asked the question in all their minds.

Ellen crossed her arms over her chest, warming her hands beneath her arms. She looked at Mandy. "Zach's coming here for Thanksgiving."

"Daddy's coming home! Yeah!" Bonnie jumped up and down, clapping, her face wreathed with joy.

Doubt darkened Mandy's anticipation of the holiday. Would it end up the wonderful experience Bonnie expected?

❧

Tension filled the Christmas barn the next two days. Zach's news tarnished the joy with which Mandy had looked forward to her only day off until Christmas.

Beth declared firmly she wouldn't see her father. She continued that assertion all the way through to Thanksgiving, but Mandy felt certain she saw a sense of excitement and hope in the girl's eyes that wasn't due to anticipation of a turkey dinner.

Grandma Tillie invited Mandy, Ellen, and the girls to join her, Grandpa Seth, and Jason for Thanksgiving. Ellen tried to decline, explaining Zach's uninvited presence. "We'll go to a restaurant," Ellen said, wrinkling her nose. "Less chance for him to make a scene and less excuse for him to hang around too long. I haven't said anything negative about his visit to the girls, but from past experience I don't expect him to get through an entire day in a pleasant mood."

Grandma Tillie brushed aside Ellen's excuses. "He won't dare act up in front of Seth and Jason. Seth and I want you to spend the day with us. We won't take no for an answer."

In the end, Ellen agreed. "Actually, it's a relief knowing we won't be alone with him," she admitted to Mandy after Grandma Tillie left. "It's not that I'm afraid of him. He's not a violent man. But he does have a talent for knowing just the right thing to say to cut a person's heart. He seems to enjoy hurting people with words."

As a writer, Zach should understand the power of words, Mandy thought. Perhaps he did. Perhaps he realized words could maim and kill as effectively as guns or knives. How had life wounded him that he felt the need to use words against the woman he'd once loved and against his own children? She doubted Ellen had any desire to extend the man sympathy at the moment, so she only said, "How sad that he chooses to use words to harm instead of to heal and encourage."

❧

"Mommy."

The bed shook.

"Mommy."

Mandy fought to stay in her dream, to stay in the warm though unreal shelter of Jason's arms, the wonderful world of his kiss.

The bed shook again. Mandy groaned and forced her eyelids open. Bonnie, wearing her Barbie nightgown, stood beside the bed Mandy and Ellen shared. A frown furrowed the girl's usually smooth forehead as she stared at her mother. "Wake up, Mommy." Bonnie pushed both hands against the mattress, trying to make it bounce.

Ellen rolled onto her back, her eyes still closed. "What's the matter? Are you or your sister sick?"

"No, but—"

"Then go back to bed."

Mandy agreed wholeheartedly though silently.

"It's Thanksgiving, Mommy."

"I know." Ellen's murmur grew fainter. "That's why we can sleep in."

"But Daddy's coming. We need to get dressed."

"He won't be here for hours and hours, Pumpkin."

"Are you sure?"

"I'm sure." Ellen opened her eyes to narrow slits and glanced at Mandy. "He hates morning. He thinks dawn is synonymous with noon."

"Maybe Daddy will get up early this morning 'cause he's excited to see us."

Ellen groaned and pulled her pillow over her face.

Mandy chuckled. "I think your daughter inherited her persistent streak from our mother. Remember how she woke us up when we were kids?"

Ellen groaned again. "Don't remind me."

"How? Tell me how," Bonnie demanded, leaning against the bed.

Mandy stretched her arms toward the ceiling. "She'd sing to us. A good-morning song. Something about dancing all night."

Bonnie climbed onto the bed, a mischievous gleam in her eyes. Pushing herself to her feet, she started jumping. Her hair, mussed from a night's sleep, bounced in brown curls on her flannel-covered shoulders. "Good morning. Good morning. Good morning."

No melody tied her song together, but it obtained the desired effect. Ellen pushed her pillow off her face and grabbed Bonnie's legs. The girl dropped giggling to the mattress between Ellen and Mandy.

Ellen gave Bonnie a hug. "I give up. Go pour us some orange juice. I'll be out in a minute."

"Okay." Bonnie climbed over Ellen and slid off the bed. The girl started toward the door, then rushed back and planted a kiss on Ellen's cheek. "I love you, Mommy."

"I love you too, Pumpkin."

Bonnie skipped away with a wide grin.

Mandy pushed back her covers and got up, still reluctant to leave the warmth and comfort of bed behind for the day. Ellen climbed out of bed too. They straightened the top sheet of lavender-colored flannel, then pulled up the violet-spattered eyelet comforter.

As they plumped the pillows, Ellen said, "This is one Thanksgiving Day I'm not looking forward to."

"I know." The thought of Zach's expected appearance made Mandy's stomach queasy. It must be worse for Ellen. "But a day can't be all bad that starts with a wonderful little girl like Bonnie saying she loves you."

Ellen's smile chased away the tension in her face, softening her features. "I guess it can't at that. I'm pretty blessed, aren't I?"

Mandy nodded. She felt blessed herself with Ellen and the girls such an integral part of her life.

As Mandy showered, she hummed her mother's good-morning song and turned her thoughts to the day ahead. In spite of Zach, she looked forward to the day. After all, she was spending it surrounded by people she loved: Ellen, the girls, Grandpa Seth, and Grandma Tillie.

And Jason. She and Jason hadn't celebrated a holiday together in more than eight years.

"Okay, so Jason and I aren't actually celebrating Thanksgiving together," she admitted, lathering the shampoo in her hair. "Not like a couple. But we'll be in the same place with people we both care about."

Definitely something to be thankful for. Her heart expanded in sweet anticipation.

twelve

Grandpa Seth and Grandma Tillie's home had stood watch on the mountainside for 130 years. It wasn't the old-fashioned architecture or comfortable furniture passed down through the generations which struck Mandy most each time she entered the house. Rather, it was the warmth and love that filled the large, square rooms and settled about her spirit like a soft, well-loved shawl.

Mouthwatering aromas of roasting turkey and baking pumpkin pies greeted Mandy, Ellen, and the girls when they arrived in late morning. The girls carried the toys they'd brought into the living room to play with beneath Grandpa Seth's watchful eyes while the women finished preparing the meal.

The large country kitchen with its cheery yellow walls allowed Grandma Tillie, Mandy, and Ellen to work without crowding each other. Pots and pans filled with potatoes, carrots, green beans, and cranberries covered all four stove burners.

Grandpa Seth's great-great-grandmother's woodburning stove still stood against one wall, but it was only used in emergencies when electricity fell victim to mountain storms. Grandma Tillie kept the stove's cast iron gleaming. A huge old graniteware coffeepot sat on a burner like a proud watchman.

Mandy, still humming the morning song, stood at the white rectangular table in the middle of the room and sliced celery for the relish tray. The fresh smell of soap and water and the enticing scent of aftershave warned her of Jason's presence before she heard him. The sense of his nearness sent delightful tingles along her nerves.

He reached around her and picked an olive from the crystal tray in front of her. "Happy Thanksgiving, Mandy."

The simple action provoked a sweet memory of the way her

father loved to come up behind her mother when she worked in the kitchen, give her a hug with one arm to divert her attention while with the other he stole a tidbit from whatever she was preparing.

"Happy Thanksgiving, Jason." She turned to smile at him and caught her breath softly. He'd changed from his usual jeans and flannel shirt into gray chinos and a black polo sweater.

Ellen, holding a jar of spiced apple rings, stopped beside them. "You clean up good, J. P."

He certainly does, Mandy thought.

"You ladies don't look so bad yourselves."

"Why is it compliments are so hard to recognize coming from you? 'Don't look so bad.' You couldn't say we look movie-star gorgeous?" Ellen held out the jar of apple rings toward him. "Here. Make yourself useful."

He took the jar. "What am I supposed to do with this?"

"Take the rings out of the jar and put them on the relish dish." Ellen explained slowly and distinctly as if speaking to a young child. "And use a fork, not your fingers."

Mandy grinned. Ellen and Jason had always teased each other this way. Mandy retrieved the jar from Jason. "You know better than to put him in charge of any kind of food, Ellen. There won't be any apple rings left for the rest of us if he gets a chance at these." She slapped lightly in the direction of Jason's fingers as he reached for another olive. "See what I mean?"

Jason shook his hand in pretend pain. "You are two tough ladies in a kitchen."

"Someone needs to guard the food," Mandy retorted, "and make sure others get to eat today." She enjoyed the everyday ordinariness of simple exchanges like this with him.

Beth and Bonnie wandered into the kitchen. Bonnie held up a folded piece of white typing paper. "Look what I made for my daddy, J. P."

Jason looked at the paper. "Hey, it's a turkey."

"It's a Thanksgiving card," she explained.

Beth shook her head. "He can tell that, Silly."

Bonnie ignored her. "I made it myself. I held my hand on the paper and drew around my fingers." She pointed to the colorful crayon turkey. "See? My fingers made the tail and my thumb made the head."

"Wow. I'm impressed."

Jason's compliment brought a grin to Bonnie's face.

Beth shrugged her shoulders and brushed at her blond hair with one hand. "I learned how to do that in kindergarten."

Bonnie's grin faded.

"You must have attended more advanced kindergarten than I did," Jason told them, "because I never learned how to do this."

Bonnie's grin returned. "Do you think my daddy will like it?"

"Of course he will." Jason handed the card back to her. "He'll think you're a great artist."

Mandy's heart caught in an unexpected sweet pain at Jason's loving attitude toward the girls.

Beth walked to the counter where Grandma Tillie stood counting serving bowls. "Can Bonnie and me help, Grandma Tillie?"

The older woman wiped her hands on her terry-cloth apron and looked around the kitchen. "The dining room table isn't set yet. Come along. I'll show you where everything is." She took a couple steps and stopped. "I forgot to iron the tablecloth. Ellen, would you do that?"

As the four left the kitchen for the diningroom, Mandy heard Bonnie ask, "Will Daddy be here soon?"

Jason leaned back against the kitchen table and glanced at the oak wall clock. "Eleven-thirty. Surprised Zach isn't here yet. Thought he flew into Winston-Salem last night."

Mandy nodded. "That was his plan, and Winston-Salem is only a little over an hour from here."

"If he doesn't show up after promising those kids. . ." Jason stopped without stating the implied threat.

"I don't know whether to be angry with him for keeping them waiting or glad he's arriving late so there's less time we need to spend with him."

Jason grinned. "Why, Mandy. That's about the meanest comment I've ever heard you make."

She felt her cheeks heat. "Are you implying that I am a Pollyanna?"

"I think that's a pretty apt description." He reached for another olive.

"Just because I don't think it's necessary to say unkind things about people doesn't mean I'm not realistic."

"True. You must be realistic about business. That's a great store you created."

She debated a moment whether to allow him to so easily change the subject and decided carrying hurt feelings over such a small matter wasn't worth the effort.

He reached for a piece of celery. She brushed his fingers away. "One little compliment doesn't entitle you to more food."

He chuckled and crossed his arms over his chest. "I was surprised when Gram said you'd be spending Thanksgiving with us. I thought you'd spend it in Asheville with your folks."

Did he resent her spending the holiday with his family? She searched his eyes but saw no anger there. "My parents moved to Texas two years ago. My brother and his family live in San Antonio. My parents like it there, and my brother's family gave Mom and Dad the excuse they were looking for to move. They spend Easter with Ellen and me, and Thanksgiving and Christmas with our brother's family."

"Do you miss living near them?"

"Not as much now as I did at first. I don't feel cheated that they've chosen to live closer to my brother than to me and Ellen, if that's what you mean. In this day and age, it's easy to travel. I plan to make a trip to San Antonio this winter when the Christmas rush is past. Speaking of distances, how are your partners in New York getting along without you?"

She instantly regretted her question. His face looked suddenly tired.

"Neal, the senior partner, likes to complain whenever we talk, but I'm not worried about the firm. It's not like I'm the only knowledgeable player."

"No, of course not," she murmured. "Grandpa Seth said you were working on a major merger at the time of his heart attack. He's concerned that because you came here, your client didn't receive the best representation."

"The client's case turned out fine." Jason straightened and wandered toward the stove.

Mandy wondered whether he moved so she couldn't see his expression.

"I spent a lot of time on the phone and computer to the office until the deal was done," Jason admitted.

Worrying about his clients in addition to putting in fourteen- to eighteen-hour days here can't be good for him.

Ellen bustled back into the room. "Every five minutes all morning it's been 'How much longer until Daddy's here?' "

"Zach knows you're here at Gram and Gramps, right?" Jason asked.

"He knows. I even gave him the phone number here and told him dinner is at noon. He's just acting his usual unreliable self."

"There's still a few minutes left before twelve," Mandy tried to reassure her. "Zach will probably drive up right on the hour."

He didn't.

"We'll just keep everything warm." Grandma Tillie turned down the heat beneath the potatoes. "Won't hurt things to cook awhile longer. Won't be the first time we didn't sit down to dinner right on the minute we planned."

"Does Zach carry a cell phone?" Mandy asked.

Ellen shook her head. "I don't know."

At twelve-thirty, they still waited. Ellen's temper grew shorter. Everyone's stomachs grew hungrier.

Ellen called Zach's California number. "Just in case he

never left." No answer.

Mandy hurried back to the Christmas barn and checked their E-mail and answering machine. No message.

By one o'clock, Zach still hadn't arrived. Bonnie's eager expression was changing to fear of disappointment. Beth's I-don't-care attitude had blossomed into outright belligerence.

Seated at the kitchen table with Grandma Tillie and Ellen, Mandy looked over at her sister. Ellen's lips were tight with fury.

Jason sat down beside Mandy. She gave him a tired smile, but his attention was on Ellen. "I think it's time we made some phone calls."

Anger drained away from Ellen's face, leaving it pale. "You think Zach's been in an accident?"

"I think it's possible. He lived in this area for years, so it's not likely he's lost. The weather's good for travel—no rain, snow, ice, or fog—but accidents happen."

Ellen took a deep breath and nodded.

Jason turned to his grandmother. "The girls are pretending to watch television with Gramps. Why don't you make sure they stay there? It's probably best if Ellen calls from the office. Less chance the girls will overhear her there."

Mandy kept her arm around Ellen's waist as they followed Jason. An office window looked out over a pattern of Christmas tree plantings on a distant hill. Maps of cities covered a large bulletin board on one wall, red tacks marking Christmas tree lots. The opposite wall held maps of the Always Christmas Farm, with indications of the types of trees and stage of growth in each area.

Jason first verified the plane Zach had been scheduled on had arrived on time. The state patrol knew of no accidents with a man of Zach's description. Jason's last call was to the local hospital. When he hung up, he shook his head. "Zach's not there."

Ellen, looking dejected, sat in the green leather desk chair, swinging it back and forth with a push of her foot.

Jason leaned against the old oak filing cabinet beside the desk. "I suppose we could call the California state patrol and see if Zach was in an accident there. Or call all the hospitals in Winston-Salem."

"Sounds like a lot of work," Ellen said.

Mandy stared at the ceiling. There must be a way to find him. "Where are his parents living now?"

"Iowa. Not exactly on the flight pattern from Los Angeles to Winston-Salem," Ellen clarified with a hint of sarcasm.

"We called our parents this morning," Mandy reminded her. "A lot of people call their parents on holidays."

Ellen stopped swinging the chair. "Zach does usually call his parents on holidays." She stood up. "I'll go down to the barn and get their phone number."

Jason dialed 4-1-1. "It's quicker to dial information." He handed Ellen the cell phone.

Mandy sent up a silent prayer as Ellen said hello.

When the call was over, Ellen set the phone down with exaggerated care. Then, fingertips on the top of the desk, she looked from Jason to Mandy. "Zach's spending Thanksgiving with his agent's family, who kindly invited him to join them since he hasn't got family in the area."

Her voice was sweet. Too sweet. A blowup Mandy could understand, but this? "Ellen?"

Ellen gave the desk chair a shove. It rolled across the room. "He could have called and told the girls something else came up and he's sorry—horribly sorry—to miss Thanksgiving with them."

Mandy slipped off the desk and slid her arm across Ellen's shoulder, wanting to give her a hug and share her pain.

Ellen stepped away and stormed to the door. "Buckshot is too good for that man."

Mandy felt Jason's hand on her shoulder and was grateful for it. She knew her sister was trying to stay strong, but Ellen's rejection of her sympathy hurt. Mandy tried to put it aside. Ellen and the girls' emotions were the ones that mattered now.

Ellen yanked the door open. Then she closed it slowly and leaned her forehead against it. "What am I going to tell the girls?"

thirteen

Anger at Zach's selfishness surged through Jason's veins. He crossed the room and cupped his hands about Ellen's shoulders. "Tell them the truth, at least part of it. Tell them Zach didn't make it because of business."

"They'll wonder why he didn't call."

"Say they can call him later. If you want to, that is."

"Want to?" Ellen gave a shaky imitation of a laugh. "I never want to speak to him again. But I won't stop the girls from calling him."

"Shall I go with you to tell the girls?" Mandy asked.

Ellen shook her head. "No. But I'd appreciate it if you'd tell Grandpa Seth and Grandma Tillie." Ellen gave another shaky laugh. "I'm sure Grandpa Seth is more than ready to eat his Thanksgiving dinner."

While Ellen spoke with the girls in the living room, Jason and Mandy told Grandpa Seth and Grandma Tillie in the kitchen. Anger and frustration registered on Grandpa Seth's bearded face. "Some men never realize it's a privilege to be a father and to spend time with their children."

Grandma Tillie, her lips tightened into a straight line, patted her husband's arm.

They're thinking about Mom, Jason realized. *Thinking how they'd give anything for another few minutes with their only child. I'd give anything for a few minutes with Mom too.* The remembrance made Zach's behavior appear even crueler.

"Guess it's time to get dinner on the table." Grandma Tillie picked up quilted, scorched hotpads. "Expect your heart won't keep you from carving the turkey, Seth." At the oven she turned around. "Those young-uns will be upset enough without lookin' at any more long faces. Let's try to keep things cheerful for them."

By the time the serving pieces were all on the table, Bonnie had cried herself out, though her eyes appeared swollen and red-rimmed. Beth's eyes looked suspiciously bright, but Jason doubted she'd allowed herself to cry over her father's change in plans. She carried the I-don't-care-what-my-Dad-does-he-can't-hurt-me look with which Jason had become familiar. She was one tough little kid. On the outside anyway.

"I'm sorry if your dinner's ruined," Ellen apologized to Grandma Tillie while everyone seated themselves.

"Don't you worry yourself about it. A little gravy and a lot of love makes anything taste good," Gram assured.

Mandy sat beside Jason, and when everyone held hands and repeated grace together, it gave Jason special pleasure to hear her sweet voice join with his in thanksgiving. It also brought back memories of holidays past he and Mandy had spent with Gram and Gramps, and a painful lump filled his throat when he acknowledged that today he and Mandy weren't here as a couple. He tried to push the pain away. He and Mandy had at least formed a tentative friendship in the last few weeks. He should be satisfied with that and grateful for it.

Gramps's mildly outraged voice broke into Jason's thoughts.

"What are you doing, Woman? I can dish up my own food. Been doing it since I was old enough to hold a fork."

Gram, seated beside Gramps, put a tablespoon of mashed potatoes on his plate. "I've watched you dish up your own food for over fifty years. I know the way you pile up the most fattening food. Need to watch out for those arteries of yours."

"I'll watch out for my own arteries." Gramps grabbed the serving spoon.

Gram gripped the spoon harder. "We've seen how well that worked out. Landed you flat on your back in the emergency room."

"I'm not apt to forget it. Let go of that spoon. You've fed

me nothing but vegetables all week. It's Thanksgiving. One decent meal isn't going to put me back in the hospital."

Jason chuckled. "Might as well give in, Gramps. She's bound and determined to keep you around."

"Even though you're ornery as a mule." Gram released the spoon and the bowl of potatoes. "Just remember what the doctor said and see that you watch your portions."

"Like living with a nurse," Gramps grumbled. "Where's the candied yams?"

"Didn't make any." Gram handed him the turkey platter. "Enough other food today that's bad for your heart."

"Hardly seems like Thanksgiving without candied yams. Suppose you didn't make pumpkin pie and whipped cream either."

"Did so. Don't be thinking you'll get more than a sliver of dessert, though. Consider yourself fortunate your Thanksgiving dinner isn't turnip greens and nothing more."

Jason, Ellen, and Mandy broke into laughter. Jason knew Gram's nagging was her way of telling Gramps she loved him, and Jason knew Gramps knew it too.

"Why are you all laughing?" Distress and fear filled Beth's eyes. "Are you going to get sick again, Grandpa Seth?"

Seeing her terror, Jason disciplined his grin and saw Mandy and Ellen do the same.

Gramps handed the turkey platter to Gram and turned his full attention to Beth. "I'm going to do my best not to get sick again. It's true I need to eat healthy foods, but one Thanksgiving meal isn't going to hurt me, and Tillie knows that." He grasped Gram's hand. "Isn't that right?"

Gram darted him a sharp glance and pressed her lips together hard before answering. "Yes, but it's best to set good eating habits right off."

"I'll be careful." He turned back to Beth. "Another thing I'm doing to make my heart healthier is exercise. Jason bought me an indoor bike and a treadmill. Maybe you'll come up and exercise with me sometimes."

Beth's face brightened. "Okay. That sounds like fun."

"Can I exercise with you too?" Bonnie asked.

"Absolutely."

The girls grinned at each other.

Jason glanced around the table as the group ate and visited, watching the simple interaction between his family and Mandy's family, the sharing between generations. In New York he seldom spent time around children. His work brought him into contact with adults of every age, but he seldom saw them in their roles as parents and grandparents.

I've missed that. Missed being part of a family.

He'd dated a number of women through the years but no one other than Mandy whom he'd wanted to bring into his grandparents' home or with whom he'd wanted to raise children. Spending the last few weeks close to her only reinforced the correctness of his decision not to marry any of the other women. *A lonely thought, since marrying Mandy isn't in my future.*

He glanced across the table at Beth and Bonnie. *What was Zach thinking, leaving his family? If I had two fantastic daughters like these, nothing could tear me away from them.*

The Thanksgiving meal lived up to prior years' tradition in satisfaction in spite of overcooking. Everyone agreed they'd appreciate dessert more later.

Gram turned down Mandy's and Ellen's offers to help with dishes. "I've no intention of going from table to sink. The dishes will clean up just as well later. Go out in the living room and visit with the others. I'm going to start some egg coffee before I join you."

Mandy and Ellen wandered over to the Christmas tree, which stood in a place of honor by the front window. Gramps went from the table directly to his recliner. The girls checked on the dolls they'd left on the sofa. Jason leaned against the doorjamb between the dining room and living room and watched the others.

Mandy looked over her shoulder at the girls. "Did you

check out the Christmas tree yet?"

"Yes," Bonnie answered. But she and Beth picked up their dolls and walked over to the tree anyway. Bonnie leaned against Mandy's side, gazing up at the tree, and Mandy gave Bonnie a hug with an arm about her shoulders.

He'd seen them that way together a dozen times in the last two weeks, Jason realized. Bonnie seemed as comfortable with Mandy as with Ellen, her own mother.

Beth held herself more aloof. Even when she ventured near Ellen, she kept a little distance. Trying to protect herself. She might take someone's hand or allow them to touch her or hug her for a minute, but she never leaned into someone with complete abandon the way Bonnie leaned against Mandy now. And Beth didn't allow a hug to last for long.

He recognized himself in her. He suspected Beth recognized herself in him too, though likely not at a conscious level.

Bonnie made herself more vulnerable. Bonnie trusted. And in doing so received both the physical and emotional comfort that Beth denied herself. Mandy and Bonnie were a lot alike that way.

Gram stopped beside Jason in the doorway. They stood together in amiable silence, watching the others.

A soft *plunk-plunk-plunk* sounded from the kitchen. Jason grinned at Gram. "Sounds like you got the coffee started." Gram always preferred egg coffee perked in a large old pot on the stove to coffee made in a modern coffeemaker. "You spoiled me with your egg coffee. Specialty coffees and coffee shops are big with my coworkers in New York, but I'd put your coffee up against any of the specialty coffees."

"Flatterer."

He could tell his comment pleased her.

She inclined her head to indicate the group in front of the tree. "They're a nice little family, aren't they?" She spoke low, her voice not meant to carry beyond the two of them. "I'm glad Ellen and the girls moved in with Mandy. Gives her someone to wrap her heart around."

Jason glanced from Gram to Mandy in surprise. Did Gram mean that Mandy might be lonely without her sister and nieces? Mandy always impressed him as the least lonely person in the world. Her sincere interest in others drew people to her, created a circle of warmth and welcome.

"I know you must feel Seth and I betrayed you," Gram continued, "letting Mandy move into the barn and us not telling you. But it's been good for us, having her there. Until she moved in, I didn't realize how quiet things had grown around here after you left."

Guilt slipped into Jason's chest with her words. She and Gramps had lost their only daughter, taken him into their home, then lost him when he moved to New York. For family oriented people like Gram and Gramps, that was a lot of loss. The guilt twisted tighter. What could he do? His career was in New York.

"I don't mind that you let Mandy move into the barn. Just don't expect us to get back together." He darted a glance across the room at Mandy, reassuring himself no one but Gram could hear him.

"Don't expect anything," she retorted. "But you can't keep me from praying the good Lord brings a woman into your life for you to love."

Jason grinned. "Hope that prayer's answered. Just as long as the woman loves me too."

"So what's not to love?"

"A little prejudiced in my favor?" He gave her a one-armed hug. "It's nice to spend time with you and Gramps again."

"It's nice to have you here again."

"Say, girls."

Jason and Gram quit talking at Gramps's attempt to gain Bonnie's and Beth's attention.

"Can you tell what kind of tree that is, girls?" Gramps leaned forward in his recliner and rested his elbows on his knees.

"I think so." Beth gently touched the needles. "Is this a Fraser fir?"

Gramps smiled. "Is that a guess, or do you have a reason for saying a Fraser?"

"J. P. taught us to look at the needles. These needles are green on top and silvery underneath. I think that's what he said makes it a Fraser."

"You're right. Very good," Gramps approved.

Beth beamed.

"How old are you now?" Gramps asked.

"I'm eight. Bonnie is six."

"You know, when Jason was a boy, he loved Christmas trees. He'd follow me all over the farm, just like a puppy, right on my heels all the time."

The girls giggled.

"Like a puppy?" Bonnie repeated.

"Just like my hound dog, Butch, used to do. Jason was a right smart boy. He could identify every kind of fir and pine tree on the place by the time he was five."

"That's littler than me." Bonnie pointed to her chest.

Beth sat on the arm of Gramps's recliner. "Tell us more about J. P. when he was a boy."

"Let's see." Gramps rubbed his fist across his bearded chin and appeared deep in thought. "There's the time he ran away."

Jason burst into a laugh. "I never ran away. Where'd you come up with a tall tale like that?"

Beth grinned at him, then turned to Gramps. "Did J. P. run away?"

"Seemed like. It happened on a cold November night."

"This is November," Bonnie interrupted, coming to sit on the floor in front of the recliner.

"That it is," Gramps agreed. "Jason and his parents had dinner with us. After dinner we adults sat around drinking coffee and visiting, the way adults tend to do."

The girls bobbed their heads and gave matching smirks, as if to say, "Yes, that's what adults always do."

"It was dark, it being evening and all. Jason was just a little whippersnapper."

"Whippersnapper." The girls repeated the word, exchanging grinning glances.

"Yep, just a wee tyke, no more than three years old. We thought Jason was in this very room, playing with his trucks—he especially liked a big yellow dump truck. Filled it with small Christmas trees a friend of ours carved out of wood."

Jason caught Mandy grinning at him and shook his head, embarrassment bringing a smile to his face.

Bonnie moved to her knees, all her attention focused on Gramps. "But he wasn't playing with his trucks, was he?"

"Nope. He sure wasn't. Well, we looked through the whole house. Looked in the closets, cupboards, clothes hampers—everywhere."

"Did you look under the beds?" Bonnie asked.

"Yep, sure did. Well, by the time we got done looking through the house, we were pretty worried."

Beth picked at the edge of the chair arm. "Mom says we're always s'posed to tell her where we go. She says some people steal kids, so we need to be careful. Did you think someone stole J. P.?"

Jason felt Gramps's hesitation.

The older man cleared his throat. "No, can't say we did. We figured he went outside to find a real Christmas tree to put in his truck."

Bonnie giggled. "A real Christmas tree would be too big."

"A baby tree might fit," Beth suggested.

"A brand-new baby tree, maybe. As I was saying, it was dark out and cold. Jason wasn't wearing a jacket. We didn't know which direction he went."

Bonnie inched closer to the chair. "Were you scared?"

"Scared stiff."

Beth picked at the chair arm again. "Were J. P.'s Mommy and Daddy scared?"

Gramps darted her a curious look. "So scared they could hardly stand it." He cleared his throat. "Well, we looked in the barn and didn't find him."

"Our barn?" Beth asked.

"Yep. Wasn't a Christmas store then. He wasn't in the barn. We called our neighbors and the men who worked for us. Everyone came with lanterns and flashlights. We spread out and walked through the groves, calling out Jason's name. We walked for hours and hours. Almost all night. We had to walk slow so we wouldn't miss him, because he was little, you know."

Bonnie nodded, her eyes wide.

"Near dawn, I heard Butch howling."

"Butch your dog?" Beth asked.

"Yep. See, Butch wasn't more than about three himself at the time. He and Jason were buddies. So when Jason ran away—"

"I didn't run away."

The girls laughed.

"When Jason took off," Gramps amended, "he took Butch with him. When I heard Butch howling, I headed straight for that mournful sound. Sure enough, Butch and Jason were together. Jason was curled up snug as a bug in a rug, sound asleep beneath a Scotch pine. Butch was practically laying on top of him. Figure Butch probably saved Jason's life that night. Kept him warm."

" 'Cause Jason didn't have a jacket, right?" Bonnie asked.

"That's right." Gramps nodded. "You never saw a boy get as much attention as Jason the next day. Someone was always hugging on him: his mom or dad or Gram or me."

"Or Butch?" Beth grinned.

"Well, Butch didn't give hugs, just sloppy kisses. But we gave Butch lots of hugs."

Ellen walked across the room from the tree to the recliner. "Let that story be a lesson to you girls. There's a reason I always ask where you're going. I don't want to spend a night looking for you, scared out of my wits."

"Don't worry, Mom." Beth slid off the arm of the recliner. "Bonnie and I won't spend any nights under a Christmas tree.

Not an outdoor Christmas tree, anyway."

Bonnie stood up and hugged Ellen around the waist. "Can we have a puppy like Butch for Christmas?"

"Can you imagine what a mess a puppy would make in the Christmas store?"

"We could keep it in the loft," Bonnie suggested.

"Yes," Beth chimed in.

"It would get lonely up there, don't you think?" Ellen nodded to encourage their assent.

Bonnie shook her head. "But—"

"No puppy this year," Ellen declared.

"There's a picture of Jason from the year he ran away on the Christmas tree." Gram headed toward the tree in an obvious attempt to divert Bonnie's attention from the puppy-for-Christmas idea.

"I didn't run away," Jason repeated, following Gram.

Amusement danced in Mandy's eyes. "I don't think you're convincing anyone."

"Here it is." Gram removed a crocheted ornament with a small picture in the middle. She handed it to Beth. "That's Jason when he was three. His mother made that ornament for Jason's Christmas present to Seth and me that year." She smiled, deepening her wrinkles. "It was our favorite present."

Mandy stood between Jason and Beth, and the floral scent of Mandy's shampoo blended with the pine scent of the tree. Mandy looked over Beth's shoulder at the picture, then back at Jason. The smile in Mandy's eyes when her gaze met his was so tender, his heart felt like it flipped over.

Beth held the ornament as though it were a fragile piece of glass. Bonnie stood beside her to get a look. "That's J. P.? He doesn't look like J. P." She looked up at Jason. "You had chubby cheeks."

"Flattery will get you nowhere."

Beth handed the ornament back to Gram. "Thank you for showing it to us."

Gram hung it back on the tree. "The woman who made it is

the same woman who makes the crocheted ornaments you sell in your store, Mandy."

"I don't recall selling any photo ornaments like this among her items."

"Why don't you have pretty ornaments like we do at the Christmas barn, Grandma Tillie?" Bonnie asked. "All your decorations are old."

"Bonnie, you apologize," Ellen scolded.

"I'm sorry, Grandma Tillie. But it's true."

Gram nodded. "It is true. I wouldn't trade one of these ornaments for a whole tree full of new ones, no matter how pretty."

"You wouldn't?" Bonnie frowned.

"No. You see, these aren't just decorations. They're memories. Each one is a memory of a special person or a special time or a special love." Gram removed a cotton-ball snowman. "Jason made this for me."

The girls grinned over their shoulders at him.

He shrugged. "What can I tell you? The world lost a great artist when I went into finance."

"Oh, right." Beth's tone let him know she didn't believe him.

Gram removed another decoration. "Jason made this angel from a toilet paper roll."

"I can't believe you kept all these things." Jason spoke over the girls' laughter.

"Of course I kept them. You were very proud of this angel at one time."

"That's because you and Mom treated everything I made like it was a masterpiece and displayed it all. I was a college freshman before I discovered I wasn't the world's next Picasso."

"All children should be so fortunate," Mandy commented softly.

His gaze followed hers to Beth and Bonnie. Mandy was right.

Jason and Mandy watched while Gram pointed out more family heirloom ornaments and explained their history to the girls. Waves of memories washed over Jason, memories of

Christmases before his parents died when he'd been too young and innocent to know how precious those times were as they happened.

"We need a tree like this."

Mandy's voice brought Jason from his memories. "There isn't space for one more tree in your store."

"Not in the store. In the loft. In our home. We need a tree Beth and Bonnie can hang their own ornaments on. Things that are important to them, not only beautiful or glittery."

"An ornament doesn't need to be made from a toilet paper roll to be special to someone. I expect a lot of the ornaments you sell will wind up being someone's treasures. Twenty years from now a grandmother will tell her grandchildren who gave her the handmade pottery ornament from your store and why."

Mandy studied his face. "That is unexpectedly sweet of you to say."

Sweet. Just the kind of compliment a man liked to hear from a woman. He shrugged. "Guess holidays put me in a saccharine mood."

Her gaze slid from his face back to the tree. He saw her eyes widen and glisten with sudden unshed tears, saw her mouth open in a soft gasp. Why? He turned to find out.

fourteen

Jason immediately recognized the cause of Mandy's shock. Gram held another ornament, showing it to Beth and Bonnie. The ornament was a wooden bench with a white-haired couple seated upon it, holding hands and gazing at each other.

His throat tightened painfully. He remembered he and Mandy selecting that for Gram and Gramps's Christmas present the first year Mandy spent with him and his family. Mandy had held it in the palm of her hand, smiling up at him. "This will be us one day. Old and gray and still holding hands. Young couples will walk past us and say to each other, 'Will we still love each other that much when we're their age?' "

He cleared his throat and tried to push the memory away. "The couple on that bench look even more like Gram and Gramps today than when we gave it to them."

"Yes, even more in love." Mandy's smile looked tight. Her pain-veiled gaze held his.

He recognized that pain: pain at the loss of their own love which began with such intensity, such hope and promise. Her pain intertwined with his own sense of loss, leaching life from his heart like two vines twining about a branch.

"Anyone ready for pie?" Gram asked.

Her question brought a chorus of affirmatives.

Jason tore his gaze from Mandy's, glad for the interruption. The dream of their love had been beautiful and powerful once upon a time. But the dream was over. There was no retrieving it. Mandy had chosen that ending.

Zach's nonarrival hadn't affected the pumpkin and pecan pies. The only complaint came from Gramps.

"You call this a slice of pie? A pine needle is bigger."

He received no sympathy.

After dessert, Gram finally agreed it was time to do the dishes. While the women cleared the table, Jason retrieved his grandfather's old chess set. It was a holiday tradition for the men to play chess after the meal. Setting the chessboard on the dining room table, Jason felt guilty remembering they hadn't played since the previous Christmas. How had he allowed almost a year to pass without visiting Gram and Gramps?

Jason was opening the oak box containing the chess pieces when Bonnie leaned against his thigh. "Will you play with me and Beth, J. P.?"

"I'd love to play with you after Gramps and I finish our chess game."

Gramps's chair squeaked as he stood up. He waved one hand in dismissal. "Go ahead and play with the girls. We can play chess later. Besides, I haven't taken my Thanksgiving Day nap yet."

Jason glanced at him sharply. "Feeling okay?" He kept his voice light with an effort.

"Fine. Something about a Thanksgiving meal makes me want to sleep like a baby. I'll just take a snooze in my recliner."

I'm overly cautious, Jason told himself, closing the box. He smiled at Bonnie. "So what are we playing?"

"House." Bonnie's grin was bright with anticipation.

Great. I gave up chess for this? Jason thought as he stood up. "I've never played house."

"It's easy." Bonnie closed her little fingers about his hand and led him to the rose-print sofa.

That flowered material always seemed so unlike Gram with her tough spirit, Jason thought. Of course, he better than most knew her heart combined that strength with gentleness and compassion. Like Mandy's heart. He'd never before recognized that similarity between the women, but he knew instantly the truth of it.

Dolls, doll clothing, toy dishes and baby bottles, some of Gram's old shoes and hats, and other paraphernalia Jason couldn't readily identify covered the couch. "It takes this much stuff to play house?"

"Yes." Bonnie nodded emphatically. "It's lots of fun. You'll like it."

Beth carefully wrapped a pink blanket around a doll which was almost too large for her arms. "Daddy didn't like to play house."

Beth's expressionless voice and face didn't fool Jason. He knew her words came from a distressed heart.

"Too bad your dad missed out on the fun."

Beth's gaze met his, and he knew he'd said the right thing. He winked at her. She grinned in surprised delight and ducked her head, giving her attention back to her baby doll.

Jason sat down cross-legged on the floor, more determined than ever to be a good sport about this change in his plans.

Bonnie handed him a doll with curly blond hair and blue eyes that closed. It wore a short white T-shirt and a diaper. "This one can be your baby 'cause it's a boy."

"Thanks." He held it by the neck with his left hand and pretended to critically study the rubber face. "What's its name?"

"Ted." A look of disgust lodged on Bonnie's face. "You can't hold him like that. He's a baby. Hold him like this."

"Sorry," he mumbled while Bonnie tried to adjust his arms.

He heard a muffled laugh and looked up to catch Mandy watching from the dining room doorway, hand over her mouth, her green eyes dancing with laughter.

"Good for you, Bonnie," Mandy encouraged after removing her hand from her grin. "It's important for a man to learn how to hold a baby."

"Hold it like this, J. P." Beth cradled her own baby doll in her arms.

He copied her, laying the doll on its back in his arms. The doll let out a "Waaaaa!" as though in protest. Jason straightened his shoulders, sure he'd mastered the simple task. "How's that?"

Bonnie propped her little fists on her almost nonexistent hips. "Haven't you ever held a baby before?"

"Not for a long time. Last time I held a baby was. . .let's

see." He frowned, trying to remember. "Beth, you were the last baby I held."

"I was?" Pleasure lit her blue eyes.

"Yes."

"As I recall," Mandy interrupted, laughter underscoring her voice, "Beth was the first and last and only baby you held."

Beth's smile grew. "I was?"

"I think so." Jason forced the words around his heart, which had taken up residence in his throat. How could Mandy remember such a minute detail from his life? Of course, he remembered everything about the time they'd spent together in love—at least, that's the way it felt.

He'd told himself all these years that she hadn't truly loved him. But would she remember so many things if she hadn't loved him as much as he loved her? The picture leaped into his mind of her tear-filled eyes at the sight of the ornament they'd picked out together for Gram and Gramps. Had he been wrong all this time? Could it be Mandy's love had been deep and true, in spite of the fact she'd turned down his marriage proposal?

Bonnie leaned against his shoulder, jarring Jason back into the present, her gaze imploring. "Didn't you hold me when I was a baby?"

Beth heaved an exaggerated sigh of exasperation. "He didn't know you then. He just met you a few weeks ago, remember?"

"Oh, yeah."

Jason chuckled again at Bonnie's disappointment. "Hey, I thought we were going to play house. Let's get this show on the road."

He gave himself to the girls' make-believe world and found himself enjoying it immensely—not the act of playing house but involving himself in the girls' imaginations and knowing his involvement increased their enjoyment.

The girls taught him how to change a diaper, how to hold a baby bottle, and how to test the milk for warmth—though of course the bottle didn't contain milk.

The girls soon tired of changing and feeding dolls, and Beth announced it was time to go shopping. He discovered this was the reason for Gram's old hats and shoes, for one evidently couldn't go to the store without dressing up properly. His ego protested loudly when he realized the girls' intention, but he stilled it and accepted a faded pale blue felt hat with a feather slid jauntily into the narrow band surrounding the rounded crown.

He did his best to act disappointed when none of Gram's awful, old high-heeled shoes fit him. He vocally admired the patent-leather monstrosities upon which the girls tried to teeter.

Too bad handbags aren't dependent on foot size, he thought, even as he accepted a blue handbag with tiny handles from Bonnie.

"It matches your hat." She looked delighted with her choice.

The girls weren't ready yet. There was plastic jewelry to don which stuck to the skin like stickers.

Jason drew the line at the pink stuff in a bottle with a golden-haired princess on the front.

"But it's perfume. It will make you smell good." Bonnie sniffed the bottle as if to demonstrate.

"It will clash with my aftershave. Where are we going shopping?"

"In the kitchen," Beth announced.

Jason swallowed a groan, but carrying the purse in one hand and the doll in the other, he gamely followed behind the girls, who teetered along on the high heels. A glance at the recliner reassured him Gramps was deep into his Thanksgiving nap and couldn't tease Jason about his outfit later.

The women's faces broke into wide grins when the threesome entered the kitchen. Jason caught the gurgles of strangled laughter.

"I loved that hat and purse when they were new," Gram told him.

"How long ago was that?" Jason asked.

"About 1950." Gram put one hand behind her head and the

other on her hip and gave a Mae West pose. "I thought I was hot stuff. That hat was the height of fashion."

The girls broke into giggles.

Mandy grinned. "Feel like hot stuff, Jason?"

He imitated Gram's pose the best he could with a doll in one hand and a handbag in the other. "The hottest."

Mandy's grin erupted into laughter.

The girls' bodies jiggled with their laughter. Bonnie wobbled on her high heels. "I–I'm going to fall," she squeaked out between giggles. She sank to the floor, which caused her and Beth to laugh harder.

Beth put her hand to her stomach. "My stomach hurts from laughing."

"Mine too," Bonnie stuttered.

Jason helped the still-giggling Bonnie to her feet.

"Smile."

Jason turned toward Mandy's command without thinking.

Flash. Mandy lowered her camera, grinning.

Great, Jason thought. *My moment of glory is recorded for posterity.*

The front doorbell rang.

"I'll get that." Jason's tossed the hat to the kitchen counter and dropped the purse and doll beside it. "I'll get you for that picture too," he whispered as he walked past Mandy.

He strode through the living room, glad to get away from the women and playing house.

Cold air rushed in when he opened the door. Tom Berry stood on the porch, a wool plaid jacket warming his body, his heavy brown beard warming his face. "Happy Thanksgiving, J. P."

"Same to you. Come on in."

Tom stepped inside just far enough to allow J. P. to close the door. "I brought the nativity—the outdoor one I told you about. You still have time to help me set it up?"

"Sure. Let me grab a jacket and tell Gram where I'm going."

It took him longer than he anticipated. When he told Gram the plans to set up the nativity on the mountainside, the girls—always ready for a new experience—piped up. "Can we go too? Please? Please?"

"If your mom says so, but. . ." He hesitated, lifted his eyebrows, and looked at the girls' feet. "Not in those shoes."

The girls turned to Ellen. "You can go, as long as you do whatever J. P. and Tom tell you," she said. "Don't get in their way. And it will be dark soon, so don't wander too far from the men."

"May I join you?" Mandy asked. "A walk and a little fresh air would feel good before we get started on supper."

Do I mind? Hardly. "Sure, the more the merrier."

"You always say that," Beth told him.

"Do I?" He shrugged. "Guess I like a crowd."

Mandy set a bowl in a cupboard and shut the door. "Where he lives, there's always a big crowd, Beth. He lives in New York, one of the biggest cities in the world."

And lonelier than this little farm on a North Carolina mountain. Maybe I do like a crowd around, Jason thought, *but not the kind of crowds I'm used to in the city. This kind of crowd—family and friends who are close to the heart.*

The truth of this thought struck him. Of course Gram and Gramps were always close to his heart. He'd tried repeatedly and unsuccessfully to put Mandy from his heart over the years. But now Beth and Bonnie had slid inside his heart too.

He hadn't time to examine the thought in depth. He took his coat, gloves, and ASU hat from a closet and made his way back to the living room and Tom.

"We've acquired some helpers," he told Tom. "Ellen, Mandy, and the girls are coming, if that's all right with you."

"Fine by me." Tom tilted his head to one side. A puzzled frown scrunched lines between his heavy eyebrows as he studied Jason's face.

"Why are you looking at me like that?"

"What are those pink things on your earlobes?"

Jason clapped his hands to his ears. The plastic sticker earrings.

Mandy chuckled behind him.

Heat rushed up his neck and over his face. He peeled the earrings off. "I was playing with the girls."

"Ah." A grin split Tom's beard. "That female influence will do it every time. Plays havoc with a man's mind."

That it does, Jason agreed silently, *in more ways than one.*

fifteen

The crisp nip in the air felt good to Mandy as she climbed out of Tom's extended-cab pickup truck on a rocky ridge overlooking a highway. Mandy recognized the road as the one which, a couple bends and half a mile farther along, ran past the Christmas barn. "Is this your land, Tom?"

"Yep. Just barely. Another fifty feet or so over, and you'll be back on Seth and Tillie's land."

Jason rested his hands on his hips and looked around. "You chose a good site. People will have a clear view of the nativity scene from the road."

Few trees dotted the hillside between the road below and where they stood near the top of the ridge. The wind raced across the mountainside undeterred, tossing Mandy's hair around her face. She tucked the strands behind her ears and turned her back against the wind.

A newly constructed platform of pine-fragrant wood stood on the uneven ground, and on the platform rested an A-frame structure Mandy knew must be the stable for the nativity scene. Inside the A-frame stood a simple wooden manger. A rectangular bundle of hay sat on one corner of the platform.

Jason nodded toward the platform. "Did you build this, Tom?"

"Yep. I worked on this project in my spare time for almost a year. Figure the platform will keep the figures from getting hidden by snow, should we get any before Christmas. Another of our former classmates who's now an electrician rigged some spotlights to light the display."

Tom pulled a heavy green canvas tarp off the items in the truck bed, revealing four statues: Mary, Joseph, the baby Jesus, and an angel.

The statues were large and heavy. Mandy, Ellen, and the

girls watched while the grunting and puffing men moved the pieces from the truck bed onto the platform.

Mandy thought how natural it seemed that Jason was here on the mountainside helping Tom. The same way it seemed natural to see him among the Christmas trees with the schoolchildren and celebrating Thanksgiving in Grandpa Seth and Grandma Tillie's home with herself, Ellen, and the girls.

Her heart caught in a little twinge, then regained its regular beat. Sometimes it seemed the years Jason spent in New York never happened, that when their gazes met across a room or in a group of people, he'd give her the smile that meant he couldn't wait until they were alone, and give her the wink that always made her heart want to laugh.

Had she made a mistake all those years ago, believing he'd never be happy in the city working in finance? Maybe she'd only wanted to believe it because she wanted to stay in the mountains and wanted him to stay too.

Mandy's attention slipped back to the present at a question from Ellen.

"Tom, the statues are beautiful. Did you make these?"

"Yep." Pleasure filled his face at Ellen's compliment.

"They are beautiful," Mandy agreed. "You've surpassed yourself with these. I don't know how you found time to make them and also make the pottery you sell, to say nothing of all the other aspects of running your business."

He shrugged his massive shoulders and looked embarrassed. "Other than work and church, there's not much else to fill my time."

"You're too modest," Ellen said. "You do a lot to help your mother and take care of the house and lawn."

He shrugged again. "She's family. Besides, neighbors and church family help out when life gets too crazy-busy."

Jason cut the twine binding one of the bundles of straw. Pulling a good-sized chunk from the bundle, he placed it in the manger.

For all the world as though he meant to make the bed more

comfortable for the stone child, Mandy thought. It brought a smile to her lips and heart. Most likely the hay was meant to ensure the statue of the baby could easily be seen rather than buried in the manger. Still, when Jason and Tom lowered the baby statue into the straw-filled manger, a lump appeared in her throat.

When Jason and Tom had the sculptures in place, Tom invited Beth and Bonnie to help spread straw on the floor of the platform. The girls scrambled up with alacrity.

Ellen leaned close to Mandy to stage-whisper, "I'll be pulling straw out of their hair and clothes for an hour when we get home." But Ellen's gentle expression as she watched her daughters work with Tom and Jason revealed that she didn't mind the thought of straw in the children's clothes at all.

"At least the girls seem to have forgotten for awhile that their father didn't show up today," Ellen continued, "between this and Jason playing house."

Mandy didn't know any words to ease Ellen's pain that she hadn't been able to prevent her daughters' father from hurting them. So Mandy simply squeezed Ellen's arm and stood silent.

The men teased with the girls while they worked. Seeing Jason with Beth and Bonnie brought out Mandy's maternal instincts and the memory of the dreams she and Jason once shared of raising a family together. Those memories made her heart heavy with longing.

Jason would make a wonderful father. She'd always known he would. It hurt deeply to think that when he became a father, she wouldn't be the mother of his children. She'd loved him for so long. Her attempts to move on, dating other men, looking for someone else with whom to share life and build a family, had been unsuccessful.

In a moment of clarity, she realized the Jason she'd loved all this time was the young man he'd been with the seeds within him of the man he was now. Those seeds were the faith and values he'd claimed and she'd believed in. Jason was no longer the man she'd loved before. In so many ways, he'd grown into the man she'd always believed he could be. Time, especially recently, had tested the values he'd claimed, and they'd stood true.

She loved the way he loved his grandparents and that without hesitation he'd taken a leave of absence from his work in the city to come to their aid. Loved the way he loved children, the care he extended to Beth and Bonnie in particular.

Jason would be a good man to share life with. Time-and-trial tested, he'd won her heart all over again without even trying. Or even saying he still wanted her heart.

Thank You for the gift of time spent near Jason again, Lord, and for allowing me to see the fine man he's become.

"What do you think you're doing?"

Ellen's sharp question brought Mandy from her reverie. She followed Ellen's glance to see what caused her outburst.

Beth was tucking her plum chenille scarf around the baby Jesus. Her face set firm with challenge, she turned toward her mother. "Baby Jesus is cold. He's only wearing that blue stone blanket-thing that looks like a funny diaper that's not fastened."

"It's not a real baby, Beth, and you know it. You insisted you needed that expensive scarf this year. You just put it back around your neck where it belongs."

"But—"

"No buts. Do it."

Beth obeyed, her face stormy.

Bonnie watched, wide-eyed and silent.

Tom moved close to the manger and picked up a large handful of hay from the floor. "I never noticed it before, but it does look like this little tyke might be cold, Beth. We'll stuff a little more hay in his bed. That will warm him up a bit."

Beth helped Tom tuck the hay around the small statue. When they finished, Beth stared at the manger, her lips in a sullen pout. "That helps some, but I think He's still cold."

Maybe it's Beth who feels cold, Mandy thought with a sad pang as the group climbed back into Tom's pickup. Cold at heart because her father didn't care enough to keep his promise and spend Thanksgiving with her and Bonnie. Didn't care enough even to call.

❧

Gram had turkey sandwiches ready when the group arrived back at the farmhouse, and after the fresh air everyone was ready to eat again.

Ellen leaned back in her chair with a sigh when she'd finished the last bite of her pie. "Well, girls, you'd better pick up your toys. We'll head home as soon as the dishes are done."

"Can't we stay longer?" Beth pleaded. "We don't have school tomorrow."

"We adults aren't as fortunate," Ellen reminded her. "The Christmas store will be jumping, and Thanksgiving weekend is a busy time for the Christmas tree business too."

Jason grinned at the girls' forlorn expressions. He well remembered how he'd hated to see holidays end when he was their ages. Still did. "What are you girls planning to do with your day off?"

"Maybe we'll put them to work." Mandy nudged Beth. "What do you think?"

Beth shrugged. "Okay."

Bonnie's eyes widened. "That would be fun. But what can we do?"

Mandy rested her forearms against the table. "I thought we'd set out Christmas cookies and apple cider for the customers. It would be a big help to your mom and me if you two kept the plate filled and served people."

Bonnie gasped in delight and sat up straighter. "Can we dress up?"

Jason pretended to be aghast. "You mean, wear Gram's hats and shoes?"

Bonnie and Beth burst into giggles.

"No," Bonnie finally managed. "Our own pretty clothes."

"Then I'll need to stop by and see you."

Their instant smiles warmed his heart, and he knew immediately he'd be stopping at the store tomorrow no matter how busy his day. He refused to pull a stunt like Zach, getting their hopes up and then not showing, even for a simple promise.

The house felt quiet and still after the girls, Ellen, and Mandy had left. Jason and Gramps finally played their chess game. Gramps won hands down and in record time.

"You're hardly any competition at all tonight," Gramps complained while Jason put the pieces back in the chess box. "Brain fuzzy?"

"Guess I'm a little tired, at that." Actually, he'd found the quiet without their visitors distracting. "Not used to a whole day away from the trees anymore."

Gramps nodded. "Get in a man's blood, those trees."

Jason's heart tightened at the truth of Gramps's statement. He hated to think how he'd miss those trees when he returned to New York. He stood up and stretched. "I'm going to check our E-mail and make certain none of our men have any last-minute problems that can't wait until morning to solve."

"I'll go with you." Gramps was on his feet in a flash.

"Didn't Doc say you were supposed to stay away from work? Isn't that why I'm here?"

"It's not work if you love what you're doing. You're taking the stress of the work on your shoulders. That's the part that has the power to hurt a man."

As they walked across the living room, a corner of paper sticking out from beneath the couch caught Jason's eye. He stooped to pull the paper out.

He looked down at a turkey in crayon colors—Bonnie's Thanksgiving card for Zach. Had she forgotten it, he wondered, or had she pushed it beneath the couch intentionally, wanting to forget the pain her father inflicted?

Jason set the card down on the table beside the sofa and followed Gramps toward the office. Frustration at his own inability to help the girls roiled in his chest. *How long does it take little girls to heal from a father's neglect?*

sixteen

The day after Thanksgiving proved as busy as anticipated. People started arriving at the Christmas tree farm's cut-your-own grove soon after eight o'clock. The number of customers grew steadily throughout the morning.

Jason didn't mind. The experience was a fun one for the families who came and fun for him and the others at the farm who provided the service.

He whistled "O Tannenbaum" as he headed for the house at one-fifteen. He'd take only enough time to grab a quick turkey sandwich for his late lunch. Gram would have one waiting for him, he knew.

His whistle cut off in surprise when he looked up and saw Beth sitting on the top step leading to the back porch. He smiled. "Hi there. Thought you'd be busy serving customers cookies and apple cider." He pointed to the long purple skirt below her jacket. "Looks like you're dressed for it."

Beth rested her forearms on her knees and looked at her fingers. "I wanted to be alone for awhile."

He started up the stairs. "I need to be alone sometimes too. You can stay here as long as you like." He moved past her. It disturbed him to see her so melancholy, but he'd respect her wish for solitary time. Besides, nothing could happen to her on the porch. When she grew cold enough, she'd go back to the store.

"I don't mind being alone with you, J. P."

He turned around and sat down beside her. "That's nice, because I enjoy your company."

She looked out over the yard, but he doubted she saw it. "You smell like a Christmas tree."

He chuckled. "Have a bit of pine tar on me."

"I like that smell."

"Me too." He hesitated. "Thinking about anything special?"

"Maybe."

He didn't push her. Almost five minutes passed before she spoke again.

"You know the stable Tom made?"

"The one we helped him set up last night?"

She nodded. "I'm thinking about that. I wonder why God let His Son be born in a stable. Why didn't He let Him be born in a hospital like other babies?"

Jason rubbed a gloved hand over his mouth and tried not to laugh. "Jesus was born a long time ago. I don't think any babies were born in hospitals back then. I don't know if there even were hospitals."

"God could make a hospital. God can do anything. The pastor at church said so."

"That's true, but it seems God usually leaves it to people to build hospitals."

"But it's not nice to leave a baby in a stable. In the stable Jesus would be cold. If God is Jesus' Daddy, He shouldn't let Jesus get cold."

Jason glanced at the thick, plum-colored scarf wrapped around Beth's neck. *So that's what this is about.* "God chose the best people He could find to look after His Son. He chose Mary and Joseph, remember?"

She nodded.

"Mary didn't let Jesus get cold."

"Are you sure?"

"I'm sure."

"Did she have a blanket for him?"

"I'm sure she did if she thought He'd need one. The Bible tells us that when Jesus was born, Mary wrapped Him in swaddling clothes."

"Are swaddling clothes like a blanket?"

"Not exactly. Swaddling clothes are strips of material that were wrapped around babies when they were little. The cloths covered most of the baby's body, so Jesus' skin wouldn't have been exposed to the cold."

He watched her face while she considered his comments.

"If I was born in a stable, my mom would have a blanket for me. She wouldn't let me be cold."

"I know."

"My daddy wouldn't care if I was cold, though."

Jason sighed. He felt completely at a loss. *What can I say, Lord? How can I help her?* "Sometimes our dads just don't know how to love us well."

"Did your daddy love you well?"

Jason hesitated. His father hadn't been perfect, but he hadn't left like Zach, and he'd never have promised to show up for a holiday and not kept his word. "He loved me the best he knew how."

"Mandy says God loves us and wants what's best for us."

"I believe that too."

"The pastor says God is our Father, like He is Jesus' Father."

"Yes."

"Would God ever divorce us, like my daddy did?"

"No, Beth. God's love is perfect. He'd never leave you."

"I think He might."

Shock rippled through Jason at her matter-of-fact tone. "People's love isn't perfect, Beth. Not even moms' love and dads' love. But God's love is perfect. I promise He will never leave you."

She considered his words in silence for a minute. "If God can do anything," she said slowly, "and He loves me, and He wants what's best for me, why doesn't He bring my daddy home?"

The walls she'd built around her heart crumbled instantly, totally. She burst into tears and hid her face against Jason's chest.

He wrapped his arms around her, rested his cheek against her head, and rocked slightly in the age-old comforting rhythm. His heart felt as though it would burst through his ribs in empathy for the dear girl. But he had no answer for her.

❧

Jason carried a heaviness in his chest through the rest of Friday and all of Saturday. Even while talking and smiling with customers picking out their Christmas trees, he carried the burden of Beth's pain.

Saturday one of the tree-truck drivers came down ill, and Jason filled in to make runs to Winston-Salem and Charlotte to restock Christmas tree lots. On the way back to the mountains after the final run, he stopped at a truck stop to refuel and grab a cup of hot coffee. A stand displaying mittens and gloves for sale caught his attention, and he bought a pair of children's gloves.

The clock on the truck's dashboard showed twelve o'clock midnight when he turned into the drive to Always Christmas Farm. Lights still glowed through the Christmas shop's windows, though he knew the store had closed hours earlier. He parked the heavy-duty truck near a tree grove with the other trucks, then walked down the hill in the moonlight to the barn, carrying the newly purchased gloves.

He knocked lightly, not wanting to wake anyone who might be asleep in the loft. In spite of the lights, it surprised him when the door opened only moments after his knock.

"Hi, Jason. What brings you here at such a late hour?" Mandy's green eyes held surprise. Fear swept it away almost immediately. She clutched his arm. "Is something wrong with Grandpa Seth? Is it another heart attack?"

"Gramps is fine. Honest."

The fright in her face subsided but it didn't completely disappear.

"I brought a donation for your mitten tree."

Her expression relaxed into a friendly, fearless smile. "At midnight?"

He explained his tree-delivery trips and impulse purchase. "I saw the lights on when I drove in and took a chance you'd still be up." He handed her the gloves. The thumbs and each finger were a different color. "I know it's supposed to be a mitten tree, but I figured you'd accept gloves too. These made me smile. I thought they might make a kid feel the same."

Mandy grinned. "They make me smile too. They remind me of Joseph's coat of many colors." She stepped back, opening the door wider. "Would you like to come in for a minute? We'll hang these on the tree."

The mitten tree, a Fraser fir he'd selected for her, stood near the counter, only a couple yards into the store. Already the branches bent beneath almost two dozen mittens, he noted in surprise. "Wow. Looks like a lot of other people donated already. You'll need another tree by Christmas. Maybe by next week."

"I hope the donations continue that strong. We won't put up another tree, though. Just remove some mittens as new donations come in." She hung the gloves over a shoulder-high branch. "This is the only pair of its kind. Adds a bright spot of color."

No lights or garlands trimmed the tree—only mittens. He liked the look.

He hadn't needed to bring the gloves down tonight, but he'd been glad the lighted windows gave him the excuse to do so. He'd just wanted to see Mandy, he admitted to himself. Just a few minutes in her serene presence would end the day on a peaceful note.

Pale blue smudges beneath her eyes showed her fatigue, and her hair was slightly but pleasantly mussed—none of which distracted from her beauty in his eyes.

"The local newspaper ran a small story the Wednesday before Thanksgiving on our tree idea," Mandy told him. "That helped a lot." She pointed at a pair of bright red mittens attached to each other by a long red string of yarn. "An elderly woman brought these in. She lives in an assisted living complex. She liked the mitten tree so much that she's organized a group of women in the complex to knit mittens to donate."

"That's great." *Just like Mandy,* he thought. Come up with a simple idea and end up with the entire community involved—and make it look almost like an accident.

"It's not an accident. It's the way it's meant to be, the way God is able to work through a person who is true to His calling on their life."

The thought came to him full blown. He pushed it away to examine later.

"After Christmas I plan to invite all the women in the knitting group out to the store for a thank-you brunch."

"They should like that." He glanced up at the clock above the counter. "Why are you working so late?"

She brushed her bangs back from her forehead in a weary gesture. "I'm restocking displays. Too busy to do it during the day."

"Something feels different in here tonight." Jason glanced around the shop. The sights were the same as always. The familiar scents of Christmas spices filled the air. "There's no Christmas music playing."

"We try to remember to turn it off after the store closes. Sometimes we forget and wake up in the middle of the night to Christmas songs. If it's a hymn, it can be comforting. If it's a rollicking rendition of 'Rock Around the Christmas Tree,' it's jolting."

"I can imagine." He pushed his hands into the pockets of his jeans. "Can you spare a couple more minutes for me?"

She darted him a curious glance. "Sure."

"It's about Beth." He leaned against the counter. "We talked yesterday. Remember saying you thought she might be angry at God?"

"Yes."

"I don't think she's angry at Him. I think Zach's abandonment of the family has broken her image of God as a father."

Mandy frowned. "What do you mean?"

"Most of her life she believed a father was someone who would always be in her life, always take care of her and protect her. Someone she could rely on for anything and everything she needed and love her unconditionally."

Mandy nodded. "Someone who'd never break his promises to her."

"Exactly. Now she sees a father as a person who is no more trustworthy than a stranger. Someone who puts his own interests above her needs. A father is someone she can't trust. So when the pastor or anyone else tells her God is her loving heavenly Father, it's not an image she finds reassuring—because her image of a father is damaged."

"Wow." It was a quiet statement more than an exclamation. Mandy leaned against the counter beside him. "My heart is telling me you're right."

"Ever since talking with Beth, a Bible verse has been running through my mind. 'Which of you, if his son asks for bread, will give him a stone?' It goes on to say that if human fathers know how to give good gifts to their children, our heavenly Father will give good gifts to His children too. Jesus tries to make us understand God's love by comparing it to an earthly father's love. Trouble is, too many human fathers give their kids stones when they ask for bread—figuratively speaking, of course."

"Millions of children must feel like Beth about God."

"Sad, isn't it? And terrifying."

"I don't mean to imply that every child of divorced parents has this issue," she clarified quickly, "or that only absent fathers neglect their responsibilities. But think how common the deadbeat dad is who doesn't pay for child support. And how many children and their fathers who've left the family grow apart until they never speak."

"The single-parent family has become commonplace—the single parent usually being the mother. A lot of kids are growing up without any father figure around. How do they understand that when the Bible refers to God as a loving Father, it's comparing Him to one of the most loving relationships a child can experience?"

"My mind is trying to grasp the implications of this," Mandy said. "I don't even know how to help Beth with it, let alone come up with a solution for millions of other children."

He told her about Beth's concern that God allowed Jesus to be born in a cold stable without anything to keep Him warm.

Mandy smiled at Beth's misconception, but sadness mingled with the smile. "That's why she walked about the shop looking at all the nativities today. I just realized that most show the Christ child without clothing and with only a narrow strip of blanket across His body."

"Not in swaddling clothes."

"Definitely not in swaddling clothes."

It seemed like old times, talking like this. When they had been dating, they discussed anything and everything, eager to learn each other's thoughts and ideas. Such discussions weren't what normally came to people's minds at the term "romance," but to him such times were as much a part of his romance with Mandy as every other part of their relationship.

He missed those times.

He forced his attention back to the present with an effort. "Driving back tonight, I passed Tom's nativity with the spotlights on it. It's striking out there on the mountain where everything else is dark."

"I haven't seen it from the road yet."

Jason pushed himself away from the counter. "It's already Sunday. I'd better get some shut-eye."

"Me too." Mandy stretched her arms over her head, stifling a yawn, then let her arms fall back to her side.

At her movement, the lights sparkled off something in her hair. "There's a piece of gold tinsel in your hair."

She reached up. "Where?"

"I'll get it." With his thick fingers, it was difficult to grab hold of the tinsel and not pull her hair. "It's tangled. This might take a minute."

Her hair felt as soft as it looked. He could smell the gentle scent of a floral-based shampoo, although she must have washed her hair close to dawn, almost sixteen hours ago. He concentrated on the tinsel and tried to ignore the way his heartbeat quickened at her nearness.

Don't think about how good her hair smells, he commanded himself. *Don't think about how wonderful she'd feel in your arms. Don't think how you want to press your lips to her hair and then her cheek and her lips.*

"I guess there's worse things a person can wear than tinsel." Mandy's voice held a laugh. "Like maybe pink plastic earrings."

"I'll find a way yet to get you back for the picture you took of me in that getup."

"And here I was sure you'd want to pass that picture down through the generations."

Jason looked down and met her teasing green-eyed glance, then dropped his gaze lower to where her lips quirked in a smile, deepening her dimples. Those lips looked too inviting. He kissed them—a light, quick kiss.

When the kiss ended, he pulled back so their lips were only a breath apart. His heart hammered against his ribs. He heard her breath coming short and shallow. He looked into her eyes. At what he saw there, he kissed her again, drawing her close in his embrace. She came willingly, leaning against him.

Her kiss was warm and wonderful. It felt exactly the same as her kisses in his memories and in his dreams.

seventeen

Mandy leaned into Jason's kiss. It was warm and wonderful. Exactly the same as his kisses in her memories and in her dreams.

She relaxed against him as the kiss deepened, rejoicing in the gentle strength of his arms. It felt so right here, as though she'd never left his arms, as though the years she and Jason had spent apart had never happened. As though God created their arms to hold each other and their lips to kiss each other's lips.

The kiss became another kiss and another. And then Jason wrapped his arms more tightly about her, resting his cheek against her hair. His chest rose and fell in a deep sigh. "Mandy."

The word was a husky whisper, filled with reverence. Her cheek against his shoulder, she breathed a soft sigh of contentment.

They stood together that way for many minutes, speaking to each other without words, heart-to-heart.

Finally Jason moved to kiss her forehead. "I'd better go."

She nodded, too filled with emotions to speak.

They walked to the door with their arms around each other. Beneath the silent brass bells, which announced all comings and goings, Mandy accepted a half-dozen more kisses and returned them in the age-old, lingering good-bye manner of lovers.

When Jason finally left, she leaned back against the door and closed her eyes, still feeling Jason with her. Deep joy filled every cell of her heart. "Thank You, Lord."

❧

Not a trace of Jason's earlier fatigue remained as he walked up the hill to the farmhouse through the crisp, pine-scented night air. His heart sang with the memory of Mandy's kisses and the sweet, willing way she leaned into his arms. He still felt her there.

When he climbed into bed, his mind continued reliving the wonderful minutes with her until reality pushed its ugly way into the memories.

"What was I thinking?" he whispered.

He planned to return to New York after New Year's. Every day—except Thanksgiving—since he'd arrived back in North Carolina, Neal had called or e-mailed at least once. Not twenty-four hours went by without a problem involving a client or case about which Jason's advice was sought.

He'd made a commitment to the company. Made a commitment to his father. He'd worked hard to reach this respected place in his career. It would be foolish and irresponsible to throw it away. His father hadn't raised an irresponsible son.

It was a God-given gift, this time back in the mountains involved in the work he'd always loved, spending time with Gram and Gramps and Mandy. He cherished every minute of it. But he couldn't chuck everything and move back here.

And he couldn't ask Mandy to move to New York with him.

He loved her more now than eight years ago. He loved the woman she'd become. He smiled into the darkness, thinking of her independent spirit, the cheerful manner in which she made her way through life without allowing problems and challenges and disappointments to trample her, the way Christ's love for others flowed so naturally from her.

He and Mandy shared a love for the mountains. He'd missed them horribly during the years spent in New York pursuing his father's dream for him. Eight years ago he'd asked Mandy to give up the mountains she loved for him. Now he knew he couldn't ask anyone he loved to give up something she loved that much—even if Mandy were willing. And what indication did he have that she was any more willing now than when he'd asked her to marry him?

He was jumping the proverbial gun, of course. Just because she returned his kisses tonight didn't mean she still loved him. Mandy wasn't the kind of woman who kissed a man unless she cared for him, but love—well, that might be a bit of a stretch.

One thing he knew for certain: There could be no more kisses. There was no place for their relationship to go if they moved past friendship. The more time they spent in each other's arms, the more painful the inevitable breakup.

He'd explain to her tomorrow. He hated the thought. It would be easier to just avoid her, but the easy way out was seldom the kindest.

He rolled over and buried his face in his pillow. He shut his mind to the memory of Mandy's kisses. The joy that filled him when he came to bed retreated, flooded out by the choice he'd made years ago to follow his father's dream instead of his own.

A thought nibbled at the edge of his consciousness. Something about following *God's* plan for his life. He couldn't get a solid hold on the thought and let it slip away.

He was wide awake but exhausted to the marrow of his bones.

Already he missed Mandy. Again.

❧

Sunday morning sunlight poured through stained-glass windows, adding to the beauty of the Advent service at the one-hundred-year-old church. Mandy sat beside Ellen in the same oak pew they always shared—sixth row back on the left side. She knew Jason sat with Grandpa Seth and Grandma Tillie in their traditional Sunday morning spot on the other side of the church, three rows farther back.

The joyous spirit of the season filled the sanctuary. The smell of beeswax candles from the altar and the Advent wreath added an additional element of warmth and comfort.

Mandy's first conscious thought when she'd awakened was of the time spent in Jason's arms the night before. She didn't know where they were headed, but at least she knew now that he still cared.

As the service ended and the congregation rose to leave,

Ellen leaned close to Mandy and whispered in a grumble, "How come you're so bright-eyed and bushy-tailed this morning when you got less sleep than I did?"

Mandy shrugged, smiling, intending to hug the secret to herself awhile longer. Then she changed her mind. The news was too lovely to keep to herself. "You know those kisses you keep asking me about?" she whispered back.

Ellen's eyes widened. "You mean you and J. P. . . . ?"

Mandy nodded, her grin growing.

"When? Where?"

"Last night. In the Christmas shop."

"I thought you were working. If I'd known you needed a chaperon—"

"We didn't, thank you very much."

"How did you two end up in the Christmas shop together?"

"I'll tell you later."

Ellen didn't look like she wanted to let it go, but she did.

The sisters exchanged greetings with numerous other church members as they slowly made their way with the rest of the congregation toward the sanctuary door. Mandy's gaze kept drifting across the sanctuary to Jason, but he was never looking her direction. It disappointed her only slightly. Other friends claimed his attention. She and Jason could talk later.

He certainly looked handsome in his obviously expensive gray suit, white shirt, and sapphire blue tie. Strange to think of him dressed in that manner every day in a fancy New York office instead of in the casual clothes he wore on the tree farm.

Mandy, Ellen, Jason, Grandpa Seth, and Grandma Tillie all reached the church vestibule at the same time. They were greeting each other when Beth, coming from Sunday school, pushed her way through the crowd to reach them.

She grabbed Ellen's arm. "Mom, guess what? We're going to do a Christmas play, and Teacher chose me to be Mary."

"That's wonderful, Sweetie." Ellen gave her a quick hug.

Mandy and the others added their congratulations.

Beth beamed at Jason. "I told the teacher I'll only be Mary

if we have those swaddle things you told me about for the baby Jesus."

"Swaddling clothes?"

Beth nodded. "Yes, those. I told her we need a blanket for Him too."

"What did she say?" Jason asked.

"She said that would be fine if I bring the blanket. I'm going to find Bonnie and tell her I'm going to be Mary." She ducked between two elderly women and disappeared.

Ellen shook her head. "I better round up those two daughters of mine. We'll meet you at the car, Mandy."

Ellen had barely left when Jason took hold of Mandy's elbow. "Okay if I walk you to your car?"

Mandy smiled at him, thrilled at his closeness. "Of course."

At the coatracks, Jason helped Mandy into her red wool coat, then put on his own long black dress coat. Mandy thought it made him look even more the successful young executive.

They stopped beside the driver's door of her five-year-old white Taurus. "This isn't an ideal place to talk," Jason started. "I'm sorry about that."

"That's all right. What is it?" Looking up into his face, she thought, *He looks tired.*

"It's. . .about last night." His lips formed a tense line.

Did he think she was upset that he kissed her? She smiled at him, trying to reassure him. "Yes?"

He rubbed his hand over his hair and closed his eyes. "There's no easy way to say this."

Her stomach clenched. "You're sorry you kissed me."

He nodded, then opened his eyes, met her gaze, and shook his head. "No, I'm not sorry. Not exactly."

"What then?"

"I truly care for you, Mandy. But I'm returning to New York after New Year's. There's nowhere for a relationship between us to go."

Nowhere to go. Mandy's chest felt as cold and bleak as a

snow-covered plateau. "So you'd rather stop before we start."

"Yes."

She swallowed the lump that suddenly filled her throat. "I suppose that's the intelligent thing to do."

"I think so."

"There's no chance you might move back permanently?"

He shook his head.

Mandy sighed, a sigh shaky with sobs she knew would demand release eventually. "I thought maybe you were reconsidering lately."

"No."

"Your work in New York—do you still do it for your father, or do you do it for yourself now?"

He didn't answer. The silence grew uncomfortable.

Mandy pulled her gaze from his face. "Is there anything else?"

"No. I just thought it only fair to tell you. . . ."

She nodded. She'd received the message loud and clear. He didn't want her back in his life. "I need to go. Ellen and the girls are coming."

She turned her back on him and opened the car door, then glanced at him over her shoulder. "You know, it's just possible it would make God happy to see you doing work you enjoy."

She climbed into the car. Tears burned her eyes. She tried to force them away. She had no intention of crying in front of the girls.

She heard Ellen and the girls calling good-byes to Jason, and then they were getting into the car. Ellen fastened her seat belt as Mandy backed the car up. "Now, about those kisses you started to tell me about—"

"Never mind. They were a mistake. Just one great big mistake."

❧

Jason struggled to enter into the jovial spirit of the season with his workers and customers the rest of the day and evening. He and Gramps didn't like that Sunday work was common in the industry, but today it helped to push the image of Mandy's pain-bruised eyes to the edge of his consciousness.

There was nothing to push the image away when he was alone in his room that night.

He forced himself to think on other topics, starting with the Christmas tree business. Always a lot of worries there. More truckloads of trees to be sent to distant lots tomorrow. Course, he'd already arranged for those trips.

Mandy's eyes slipped back into his memory.

He grimaced. The New York office had only contacted him once today. Neal apologized, it being Sunday and all. Seemed a silly apology since Neal was working, and it was Sunday in New York too.

Mandy would hate life in New York.

He shut his eyes and rubbed the palms of his hands over his eyelids, trying to rub out the picture of the pain he'd caused her.

If only he could fall asleep, he'd find freedom from her eyes for a few hours. Sleep wasn't accommodating his desire.

What else could he think about? There must be something besides work in his life.

Gramps and Gram. Ah, yes, finally something cheerful—Gramps's improving health.

His dad had never liked Gramps much. Jason hated the way his dad had ridiculed Gramps, simply because the older man found contentment in running a Christmas tree farm instead of pursuing a career guaranteed to bring wealth. Of course, the tree farm was large now and doing well financially. It was a small operation when Jason's dad met Gramps.

Jason didn't like this train of thought any better than thinking about Mandy. He sat up in bed, plumped up his pillows, and stuffed them between his back and the antique oak headboard, then turned on the bedside lamp. He reached for the Bible lying beside the lamp. If he couldn't sleep, he might as well read.

He turned to the Gospel of Matthew, searching for the verses which had nagged at his mind the last few days. He found them in chapter seven, beginning at verse nine: "Which of you, if his son asks for bread, will give him a stone? Or if he asks for a fish, will give him a snake? If you, then, though you are evil, know how to give good gifts to your children, how much more will your Father in heaven give good gifts to those who ask him!"

He sighed. It seemed to him too many fathers here didn't "know how to give good gifts to their children."

"Did your daddy love you well?" Beth's question from their discussion on the porch popped into his mind.

He loved me; he just didn't understand me. He loved the city and the world of finance and thought I should love them as much as he did. That I should love them instead of the mountains and Christmas tree farming.

I wanted bread, and he wanted to give me a stone instead.

Guilt and sorrow rushed through his chest. Guilt for thinking such a thing about the father he loved. Sorrow for believing the thought true.

The truth seared into his soul. He'd believed his father hadn't loved him because Jason didn't desire the same things his father desired. That's why he'd chosen to go into a financial career when his father died. One last, desperate attempt to gain his father's approval and love.

Father would be proud of my success. He'd think that stone he wanted for me is gold, through and through. He'd think that stone will buy me all the bread I need.

He and his father hadn't known each other at all.

He'd told Mandy that Zach's actions broke Beth's image of God as a Father. *I wonder if my image of God is warped because my father and I saw what constitutes bread and stones differently.* He didn't think so. *At least I understand that God is love.*

Jason set the Bible back on the table, turned off the light, and tried again to go to sleep.

eighteen

During the next few weeks, Mandy felt certain Jason avoided her whenever possible. That was all right with her. It took all her emotional strength to keep up a facade of cheerfulness for her customers and Beth and Bonnie.

Only with Ellen did she let her defenses down and reveal her sadness. Even then, she refused to discuss Jason with her sister.

She'd lied to herself about those kisses Thanksgiving weekend. Told herself it was okay; she didn't know where they might lead. She knew exactly where she wanted them to lead—into Jason's heart and soul for the rest of their lives.

Eight years ago it sliced her heart when Jason left. Now she'd reopened her heart to the possibility of his love and been wounded again.

At least Beth appeared more cheerful. Her upcoming role as Mary and the normal childhood excitement of nearing Christmas apparently cast her untrustworthy father into the background of her mind.

"Did you ever see anyone so excited about a nonspeaking role?" Ellen asked Mandy with a grin.

"She seems less preoccupied with Zach, anyway."

"Yes. Maybe one day she'll heal from his selfishness."

The Christmas store became more of a blessing than ever for Mandy. Her longing for Jason was ever-present, but the demands of the store kept her from burying herself in self-pity.

December passed in a blur except for two events the week before Christmas. The first was a Christmas card that arrived—looking innocent and cheery in a bright red envelope—with a stack of other cards and advertisements. Ellen spotted it at the end of a busy day as she went through the mail while Mandy checked the receipts against the register.

Ellen held the red envelope toward Mandy. "From Zach to me and the girls."

"Aren't you going to open it?"

Ellen scrunched her nose in distaste. "Suppose I better. He may be writing to say he's planning to spend Christmas with us." She slit the envelope with the letter opener, pulled out a card with a picture of Santa Claus, and opened it. "I don't believe it." Ellen's voice sounded strangled.

"What?"

Ellen handed her a wallet-sized photo. It was a picture of Zach and a woman with short brown hair.

"According to this signature, they're married."

"Married? He moves fast."

"I guess he hasn't changed his courting technique."

Mandy remembered the whirlwind romance between Ellen and Zach. "Are you okay with this?"

"I don't have another choice, do I?" Ellen's eyes flashed. "I don't mind for myself. I just hope it doesn't hurt the girls too badly."

"I guess this means he's not coming home for Christmas."

"Says they're spending it with the new wife's family in San Jose. At least the girls won't spend another holiday waiting for him to show up."

Mandy handed the picture back. "Will you tell the girls about his new wife?"

"I suppose they need to know. Maybe I'll wait until after Christmas. That news isn't exactly on their Christmas wish list."

The second event that stood out for Mandy was Jason's delivery of a burlap-bagged Fraser fir to the store. "You said you wanted the girls to have their own Christmas tree," he reminded Mandy. "I asked Beth if anyone had set one up yet and she said no, so. . ." He shrugged. "I know you prefer the live trees, so I brought this. Would you like me to carry it up to the loft?"

He placed it, at Mandy's request, in the loft's small dining area.

"We use the area in the store near the fireplace as our living room when the store's closed," she said, "but there are so many trees in the store. This one will seem more personal up here."

The girls jumped up and down in excitement when they saw the tree upon arriving home from school. Then they raced off to find and thank Jason.

Ellen insisted they wait until the store closed for the night before trimming the tree. "After all, it's Mandy's tree too. We all want the fun of trimming it." Ellen brought out red and green construction paper, children's scissors, and glue; and the girls filled the time waiting for Mandy by making paper chains for the tree.

When they grew tired of making chains, Beth asked, "Can we make cotton-ball snowmen, like Jason did when he was little?"

Ellen brought out cotton balls and improvised. Later she told Mandy, "I forgot children don't make Christmas ornaments in school anymore, the way we did when we were children."

Ellen dug out the small box of ornaments from the Christmases shared with Zach. She confided in Mandy her concern that some of the ornaments might awaken melancholy emotions in the girls, but that didn't happen. Beth's and Bonnie's favorite ornaments proclaimed "baby's first Christmas" for the years they were born.

There was no theme to the tree, as there were to those in the Christmas shop. The ornaments were a combination of sizes and shapes, some expensive and some recently handmade by the girls. It gave the children great joy, which caused Mandy to think it the loveliest tree ever.

The family Christmas tree became a constant reminder to Mandy of Jason's kind, thoughtful nature and of his love for children—Beth and Bonnie in particular. A constant reminder that one day he'd make some blessed children a wonderful father.

A constant reminder that she wouldn't be the woman sharing his life and future children.

So she poured her energy even more strongly into the store.

And, suddenly, it was Christmas Eve.

Mandy shared Beth and Bonnie's enthusiasm when the first snow of the season began around noon. The flakes were large and fluffy and lovely against the background of evergreens. Perfect for a white Christmas, yet light enough that Mandy didn't fear it might cause trouble for travelers.

She released a sigh of relief as she hung the "closed" sign on the door at three-thirty. Most likely a few last-minute customers would straggle by, knock loudly, and plead for an opportunity to take one more look for the perfect gift. Mandy knew she'd let them in as long as they didn't keep her from making it to church on time. She wasn't about to miss Beth in the Christmas play.

Ellen and the girls were already at the church, so Mandy had the loft to herself. She put on a new dark green velvet dress. It slid easily over the hips and waist, off which she constantly promised to whittle a few inches—and never did.

Viewing herself in the oak-framed standing mirror, she nodded approval. The simple, unadorned dress with its princess-cut flattered her figure and her hair. And matched the fir-green eyes Jason used to say were beautiful.

She'd reluctantly accepted Grandma Tillie's invitation to drive to the church with her, Grandpa Seth, and Jason. It seemed childish to say, "No, thank you. I don't even want to be in the same car as your grandson."

Grandma Tillie must know something had happened between her and Jason, but she hadn't asked questions. It was like her to allow people to work out their own solutions.

True to Mandy's expectation, two customers stopped by before she left for church. She warned them of her plans, but she doubted they'd have completed their shopping before midnight if Jason hadn't entered the store and announced he and his grandparents were ready to leave.

The snow was still falling when Mandy approached the car,

and she thrilled to the winter beauty. The wind was still, and she loved the *sh-sh-sh* sound the snow made as it drifted down through the trees.

Jason held the front passenger door open for her. His grandparents sat in the backseat, so she climbed into the front seat beside him.

She smiled brightly at the older couple. "Blessed Christmas." When they'd returned her greeting, she explained, "I read that in the United States before the twentieth century 'Blessed Christmas' was the common Christmas greeting instead of the 'Merry Christmas' popular today."

"How lovely," Grandma Tillie exclaimed as Jason turned onto the highway. "I think I'll adopt it myself. Is Beth still excited about the Christmas drama?" she then asked.

"I think she's looking forward to it more than she is to opening her Christmas presents." Mandy's comment elicited chuckles from the others. "She brought her favorite life-sized baby doll to use as the baby Jesus. Also a blue wool blanket that was a gift when she was a baby."

"I thought people gave girl babies pink blankets," Jason said, his gaze on the snow-covered road.

"Babies get every color blanket these days," Grandma Tillie told him.

Jason grinned. "Beth didn't take swaddling clothes?"

"Oh, she did." Mandy shook her head. "You are in so much trouble with Ellen over those, Jason."

"Me?"

"You're the one who told Beth about swaddling clothes. Beth insisted the baby Jesus in the play needs them. Ellen tore an old sheet into strips and told Beth to use them for swaddling clothes. What the well-dressed baby doll wears in a Christmas play."

Gramps spoke up from the backseat. "Is Zach going to delay our Christmas dinner tonight?"

"Seth." Gram sounded for all the world like Ellen scolding the girls.

"What? I want to know if I'm going to eat on time."

Mandy told them of Zach's marriage.

"Lousy Christmas present for Beth and Bonnie." Anger clipped Jason's words.

"Ellen told them Zach's spending Christmas in California. She's going to wait until after Christmas to tell the girls he's remarried." Mandy sighed. "Beth's class drew pictures of their families in school this week. Beth's picture includes only herself, Bonnie, Ellen, and me."

Jason scowled at the road. "So Zach's out of the picture. That man doesn't know what he's given away."

The drive into town didn't take long. When the group entered the vestibule, they found Ellen and Bonnie waiting for them. They all sat together, but Mandy was glad that Ellen's presence made it a simple matter to avoid sitting beside Jason. She knew with him beside her, she'd have been distracted from the service.

The program was simple. The Christmas story was presented through the play. The children acted out the story as it was read from the Bible. Hymns—some solos, some sung by choirs, some in which the congregation joined—introduced at appropriate places in the story added to the beauty of the service.

Mandy, Ellen, and the rest of their group sat up a little straighter when Beth came onto the stage area in front of the altar.

Beth sat down on a stool behind the manger and carefully adjusted her white robe. Moments later, the narrator read the Scripture which told how Mary "brought forth her firstborn son, and wrapped him in swaddling clothes, and laid him in a manger"(KJV).

With a solemn expression, Beth picked up her doll from behind the manger. The doll was wrapped in sheet strips.

Mandy could hear the stifled chuckles from all the adults in her group. She longed to lean forward, catch Jason's glance, and share this moment with him, but she resisted.

Beth held the doll in her arms and gazed lovingly at it, then laid it gently in the straw-filled manger. Next she picked up the blue blanket from behind the manger and spread the blanket over the doll with exaggerated care.

The drama held a strong impact, in spite of the many times Mandy had heard the story, and in spite of the funny, endearing moments provided by Beth and the other players.

When the story ended, the pastor rose and walked to the podium, bringing the congregation back from two thousand years ago to the present. He smiled out at the people. "Well. There's so little that one can add to that story."

Murmurs of agreement came from the congregation.

"But maybe a reminder of the reason for Jesus' birth isn't out of line. I read from First John, chapter four, verses seven through eleven." He opened his Bible.

" 'Dear friends, let us love one another, for love comes from God. Everyone who loves has been born of God and knows God. Whoever does not love does not know God, because God is love. This is how God showed his love among us: He sent his one and only Son into the world that we might live through him. This is love: not that we loved God, but that he loved us and sent his Son as an atoning sacrifice for our sins. Dear friends, since God so loved us, we also ought to love one another.' "

The pastor closed his Bible and looked out at the congregation. "Dear friends, this Christmas, may you go in love; may you go with God."

❧

A gust of wind tossed Mandy's muffler and tugged at her hair as she left the church with Ellen and the girls. Mandy caught her breath in surprise. Blowing, stinging snow had replaced the large, lazy flakes that had drifted down when they arrived. In the light from streetlamps she saw snow thick in the air. Almost three inches of the white stuff covered Ellen's windshield. Mandy reminded herself Ellen's car had been parked at the church an hour and a half longer than Grandpa Seth's.

"I'm sure glad you're riding back with us, Mandy," Ellen

said as she opened the back door of her car for the girls. "I hate driving in storms. Hope we don't slide into a ditch or something. I didn't bring a cell phone. Did you?"

Mandy shook her head. "No."

"There's a flashlight in the car. At least we'll have light if we need to walk for any reason."

"Cheerful thought." Mandy wished they were back at the farm, safe and sound.

A shadow came toward them through the swirling snow. It turned out to be Jason. "Roads might be slippery, Ellen. I'll follow you." Then he faded back into the storm.

The drive back was trickier than the drive into town had been. When they passed the area of the mountain where Tom's Christmas nativity was displayed, Mandy pointed it out to the girls. "See where that dim glow of lights is?"

"That's the stable?" Beth squinted, trying to see through the early evening darkness and the storm. "I can't see it."

"It's there. Probably covered with snow."

They arrived back at the farm, grateful they'd had no mishaps. Ellen parked beside Jason, near the farmhouse since Grandma Tillie had invited them to Christmas Eve dinner.

Beth zipped her doll inside her jacket before getting out of the car. She and Bonnie raced for the front door, followed closely by Mandy and Ellen. Once in the shelter of the porch, they and the Kramers brushed snow from their coats.

Jason undid Beth's plum chenille scarf and shook the snow from it. "By tomorrow there'll be enough snow to build snowmen. Let's have a contest."

"How do you have a snowman contest?" Beth asked as he settled the thick muffler back around her neck.

"We make up teams, and each team builds a snowman. You and Beth can be a team, and Mandy and Ellen can be another team, and I can be a team."

"What about Grandma Tillie and Grandpa Seth?"

"They can be the judges."

"I don't want to build a snowman," Bonnie announced,

entering the house while Jason held the door. "I'm going to build a snow lady." Her eyes sparkled with laughter. "Then it can wear one of Grandma Tillie's hats."

Once they were inside, Mandy helped Bonnie out of her jacket. "Did I tell you yet how pretty you look in your red Christmas dress with its lace collar, Bonnie?"

"Thanks. When do we open our presents?"

"Bonnie." Ellen, on her knees beside them trying to unzip Beth's coat—still extended from the doll beneath—glared at Bonnie.

Ellen's scolding-mother tone didn't disturb Bonnie at all. "What? I didn't say anything I'm not supposed to."

"I told you tonight's schedule before we went to church."

"I forget."

Mandy intervened. "First we eat the great dinner Grandma Tillie prepared for us. Doesn't it smell good?"

Bonnie put her head back and took an exaggerated sniff of the tantalizing odor of roast beef.

Ellen groaned and gave Mandy a glance filled with frustration. "What's a mother to do?"

"Then we open presents after dinner?" Bonnie asked.

"After the dishes are done," Ellen reminded. "We left the presents at the store, remember? Grandpa Seth and Grandma Tillie and J. P. are coming down to the Christmas barn with us. We're going to light a fire in the fireplace and open presents in front of it."

"I wish we were opening presents right now," Bonnie declared with a pout.

"Me too." Beth, finally freed from her jacket, grasped Bonnie's hand. "Let's go play dolls." They headed off together, Beth still carrying her doll, safe and warm in its blue blanket.

Ellen reached for Mandy's hand and gave her an exaggerated smile. "Come on. Let's go play house."

Laughing, they headed to the kitchen to help Gram.

The meal tasted every bit as wonderful as Gram's Thanksgiving feast. Gram scolded at Gramps's portions and choices, and he scolded her back for nagging—bringing indulgent smiles from the other adults. The wind howled around the corners of the old house, but the sound only added to the warm and cozy family feeling. Mandy sensed the undercurrent of anticipation in the girls, eager to open their gifts. *I'm so glad this holiday isn't spoiled for them by waiting for Zach to arrive.*

Mandy avoided looking at Jason, who sat at one end of the rectangular table, opposite Gramps, whom Mandy sat beside. *At Thanksgiving, our kisses were still in the future. Now they're already in the past, and we have no future.*

She turned her mind purposely to the conversation around her, reminding herself that Jason wasn't the only person in her heart. Every person at this table was a loved one. *And that's a blessing worth waking up for every day.*

After the meal, the adults, to the children's chagrin, decided to linger over a cup of coffee before beginning the cleanup.

"We'll never get to open presents," Bonnie complained.

"When we grow up, we're going to open presents first," Beth announced. "Come on, Bonnie. Let's go play Mary and Joseph and baby Jesus."

"Can I be Mary?" Bonnie pleaded as she followed Beth.

"You can take some towels from the bathroom for your robes," Gram called after them.

When the dishes were cleared, Jason and Gramps set up the chess set on the dining room table. Gramps grinned across the table at Jason. "Let's see whether I can whip you at this before the womenfolk get done in the kitchen."

Forty-five minutes later, the women were putting the last of the dishes away when Gramps said, "Checkmate," and ended the game, chortling. As he and Jason put the chess pieces away, Gram removed her terry-cloth apron with its holly design and smiled at Mandy and Ellen. "Well, I guess it's time we head down to your place and let the little ones at their presents."

Anticipation at the girls' excitement gave off a warm glow in Mandy's chest as she went with Ellen to tell Bonnie and Beth that The Hour had finally arrived. At the door into the living room, Mandy and Ellen stopped. Beth's baby doll lay on the sofa alongside a doll of Bonnie's, but no one was in the room.

A small frown showed Ellen's minor annoyance. "I guess they're playing in one of the bedrooms. I've told them not to go in them without Grandma Tillie's permission."

"I'm sure they aren't getting into anything they shouldn't," Mandy reassured. "They're probably looking for Grandma Tillie's old hats."

Mandy and Ellen went up the narrow old staircase together. The girls weren't in the bedrooms.

Mandy and Ellen stopped in the dining room where Jason and Gramps were discussing the successful Christmas tree season over another cup of coffee. "Have you two seen the girls?" Ellen asked.

"Not since dinner." Jason stretched back in his chair.

"I bet they're in the basement." Gram started toward the basement door. "There's an old sofa and chair down there we've never gotten around to throwing out. The girls like to play down there sometimes."

But they weren't in the basement either.

Mandy tried to push away the fear edging into her chest. "They're probably playing hide-and-seek."

"That's right," Jason joined in. "They're probably in some closet right now, giggling at the trouble they're causing us."

The adults went through the house, calling to the girls, ordering them to appear, peering into every closet and cubbyhole and beneath each bed.

The last closet Ellen checked was by the front door. When she turned from it, her white face and panicked eyes shot dread through Mandy's veins. "Their coats are gone."

Mandy glanced at the rug before the front door. "So are their boots. Maybe they decided to start on their snowmen early."

"In this storm?" Jason reached past Ellen to grab his coat. He slid it on while stuffing his feet into his boots. "I'll check the yard. Mandy, you and Ellen check the Christmas store."

The storm had blown a thin layer of snow across the porch

floor. The dim rays cast by the porch light revealed two sets of small boot prints crossing the porch to the steps. Mandy pointed to them, excitement threading through her. "Look."

A few feet from the bottom of the steps the prints were blown over. Mandy's heart sank at the unbroken snow. Their path was destroyed as surely as Hansel and Gretel's path. She cast a glance at Jason. He met her gaze, worry thick in his eyes.

Without a word to each other, Jason split off from Mandy and Ellen. For a short ways, Mandy could hear him calling the girls' names, as she and Ellen were doing. Then his voice disappeared, swallowed up by distance and the storm. *Or maybe he's found the girls. Think positive, Mandy.*

I never realized how many places there are for a child to hide in here, Mandy thought as she and Ellen investigated the barn, calling for the girls. It was maddening how much time it took.

Mandy had grabbed her cell phone before they left. No telling what the night ahead might hold.

The helplessness she felt at the growing terror she saw in Ellen's face added to Mandy's own fears. She slid her arm around Ellen's waist as they started back to the farmhouse. "Maybe Jason found them making snowmen behind the house."

He hadn't.

He, Grandpa Seth, and Grandma Tillie were pacing the living room. "Maybe we should call someone," Grandma Tillie said. "The sheriff or the police."

Mandy stood beside Ellen at the front door, her mind tossing about for ideas and coming up with nothing. Her gaze rested on Beth's doll, wrapped in Ellen's improvised swaddling clothes, and the memory of Beth's performance only hours earlier squeezed her heart.

Something clicked in her mind. The doll. Something wasn't right.

Mandy started toward the sofa, forgetting to remove her boots. Frowning, she picked up Beth's doll.

Jason came up beside her. "What is it, Mandy?"

"Beth wrapped the doll in the blue blanket." Mandy raised

her troubled gaze to Jason's. "Where is the blanket?"

"The nativity." The realization hit Mandy and Jason at the same time.

Ellen stared at them from beside the front door. "What are you talking abut?"

Jason hurried toward her. "They've gone to the nativity to cover up the baby Jesus."

"In this storm?" Ellen's eyes showed she refused to believe it. "In the dark?" She shook her head. "They'd never go without telling me. It's the one rule they never break."

Jason snapped his fingers. "The card. Did you get the card Beth made for you, Ellen?"

"She didn't give me a card."

"On the dining room table." Jason crossed the living room with long, determined strides, Mandy and Ellen in his wake. "Beth came in during the chess game. She laid a folded piece of paper with your name on it in crayon. I asked if she'd made you a Christmas card. She just smiled and left the room. Here it is." He handed it to Ellen.

Mandy noticed the Christmasy red crayon in which the card was written. No wonder Jason thought it a Christmas note. She glanced over Ellen's shoulder. The note wasn't long and was filled with scratched-out and misspelled words which would otherwise have caused amusement.

The paper shook in Ellen's hands, and her voice trembled as she read:

Mommy,

Bonnie and me are going to the baby Jesus. We took our jackets and a flashlight, so don't be scared like when J. P. was little.

Beth

Ellen pressed her fingers to her lips to stifle a sob.

A gust of wind shook the windows as the knowledge of the children's danger blew into Mandy's heart and chilled it.

nineteen

Jason pushed his fingers through his hair. It chilled him to the marrow to find his and Mandy's assumption was correct. "I should have told you about that note right away, Ellen."

"You had no way of knowing what it contained," Gram reassured him as she hurried toward the kitchen. "I'll call the police."

But Mandy had already punched 9-1-1 on her cell phone.

Fifteen minutes later a plan was in place. The sheriff was on the way out to the farm. His office was making calls to volunteers experienced with hunting the mountains for missing persons. Everyone knew without it being said that it was unlikely the girls would find their way to the nativity in the storm. They could be anyplace on the mountain.

The farmhouse already felt like a command center. Gramps had dug out detailed maps of the mountains in the area, including an up-to-date map of the Christmas tree farm. Gram found the two-way radios used on the farm before the advent of cell phones. Mandy started coffee and hot chocolate for thermoses and collected blankets from the linen closet.

Ellen made a quick trip to the Christmas store for a change of clothes for herself and Mandy and for Beth and Bonnie. "They're out there in their Christmas dresses and tights," Ellen reminded Mandy.

Jason called Tom Berry and explained the situation. After hanging up, Jason turned to Mandy and Ellen. "Tom's heading up to the nativity from his place."

A shade of relief passed over Ellen's face at the realization one more person was looking for her girls.

Gram put in a quick call to the pastor and received his assurance he'd immediately arrange a prayer chain among the congregation.

Jason put chains on the tires of the farm's Jeep and attached a trailer behind it to carry a snowmobile. He made certain there was a first-aid kit, a flashlight, and extra batteries in the vehicle.

When he finished, he returned to the kitchen where Mandy was pouring hot chocolate into a thermos. A sense of urgency made his chest hurt. "I'm heading out in the Jeep. I think it's important someone is out there looking for the girls as soon as possible."

"I'm going with you."

"Don't you want to stay with Ellen?"

"Grandma Tillie and Grandpa Seth will be with her. And the sheriff will have others here."

It had already been agreed that after the sheriff arrived, Ellen and Grandma Tillie would go down to the Christmas store to wait in case the children returned there. Grandpa Seth would remain at the farmhouse where volunteers would headquarter.

Mandy changed quickly into jeans, a turtleneck, and a sweatshirt, then slipped into her practical winter parka. Jason and Mandy carried a radio, cell phone, thermos of hot chocolate, and blankets out to the Jeep. They took backpacks in case they needed to travel by snowmobile later. Ellen handed them the set of clean, dry clothes for each of the girls.

Jason's heart contracted. He took a moment to hug Ellen. "Keep praying."

She nodded, and he felt her tears hot against his cheek.

Tom would be headed up the path he'd made from his place to the nativity, but the girls started out from the farmhouse. Jason's plan was to approach the nativity as close as possible from the roads through the Christmas groves, go beyond as far as possible in the Jeep, then take the snowmobile.

At one point, Jason reached over and squeezed one of Mandy's gloved hands in an attempt to reassure her. He wished he could give her true comfort, assure her the girls were fine and would be found safe and sound.

He couldn't even hold her hand for long, let alone calm her fears. Even with the Jeep's four-wheel drive and ability to travel over rough terrain, the way was difficult and demanded his full attention, with both hands on the steering wheel.

"I wish the girls had a dog with them, the way you had Old Butch." Mandy gave him a tight little semblance of a smile.

"Me too. Maybe we should override Ellen's veto and give the girls a puppy for Christmas, after all."

"A Saint Bernard might be a good choice."

He forced a chuckle. He didn't feel like laughing but appreciated her attempt at humor. "Can you imagine one of those in the Christmas store? Its tail would take out every Christmas tree in the place."

She gave him a small smile, then turned her gaze back to the windshield. "I've always liked a white Christmas, but I'd be just as happy without one this year."

Jason drove slowly, and they both tried to watch for the girls as they went along, but it was almost impossible to see anything but shadowy, lumpy shapes in the curtain of snow. They kept the windows partially down and stopped about every hundred feet to call to the girls and listen intently for an answer they never received. He sent prayers up constantly and knew Mandy did the same.

At one point they received a call on the radio from the sheriff, who'd arrived at the farmhouse. Jason told him where they were and reported they'd seen no sign of the girls. The sheriff told him the Highway Patrol was closing the highways and asked him to keep in touch.

When Jason could go no farther with the Jeep due to the thick growth beneath the snow, he stopped. "I figure we're within a quarter mile of the nativity," he told Mandy. "The snowmobiles are too noisy. If we walk, we can keep calling for the girls and have a chance of hearing them respond."

"Maybe Tom has already reached the nativity," Mandy said. "Maybe he's found the girls."

"Maybe."

"If he'd found them, he'd let the sheriff know, wouldn't he?"

"Tom took a cell phone with him, but he doesn't have a

radio. He might not be able to keep in touch with the sheriff all the time. There are dead-air places in the mountains where the cell phones don't work, as you know."

They packed the thermoses, blankets, phones, first-aid kit, compass, extra batteries, and children's clothes into the back-packs and started out on foot. They each carried a flashlight, and Jason carried the radio in a holster over his shoulder.

The trees cut the force of the wind, but it was still hard going uphill through the storm, the tangled underbrush and rocks beneath the snow making their footing tricky. Jason and Mandy held hands as they trudged along.

His admiration for her grew. She was a trooper. No complaints from her at the conditions, though he could hear her labored breathing. The chill bit at his cheeks, and he pictured the girls' legs protected only by tights and high boots. He was certain Mandy had similar thoughts, but she didn't voice them. Likely she felt as he did, that expressing their fears wouldn't do any good. Better to put all their energy into trying to find the girls.

Twice he reconnoitered and changed their direction, and still he wondered whether they were headed the right way. Would they become lost and not find the nativity until the storm let up? He sent up a prayer of gratitude when Mandy leaned close and said, "There it is." He followed the direction she pointed with her flashlight, and saw a dim glow farther up the hillside.

Their pace quickened. They resumed their pattern of calling for the girls, listening, and calling again.

Soon they reached the nativity. The wind was stronger, coming up the ridge from the highway, which Jason knew lay below, though they couldn't see it. He climbed onto the platform and flashed his light around. Disappointment cut through him like a knife blade. He hadn't realized the extent to which he'd hoped to find the girls huddled in that make-shift stable in the hay behind the statues.

He concentrated the light on the manger. Snow mounded

over the statue of the baby Jesus. No blue blanket covered it.

Jason jumped down off the platform. "Not there," he announced to Mandy unnecessarily.

Mandy shone her light beneath the platform, which stood two feet off the ground. They both bent down to look beneath it. The girls weren't there either.

A man's shout greeted them as they straightened up. It was Tom Berry, arriving on foot at the top of the rough path he'd cut through the woods for his truck.

It took only a couple minutes to exchange information. Tom's truck had become stuck a ways down the mountain, in spite of the chains on his tires. He'd seen no sign of the girls, though he'd kept a close watch and called for them regularly.

Jason pulled the radio out of his holster and called in to make his report to the sheriff. He slid an arm around Mandy's shoulders and pulled her close while he talked. The transmission crackled and the conversation broke up, but he was able to make out most of it. The sheriff explained a large group of volunteers had arrived at the farm and were ready to head out in an organized search pattern.

Jason's chest ached unbearably. The chances hadn't been great they'd find the girls here, but he'd kept a fierce hope up just the same. Now the area to search had expanded exponentially. An eight year old and a six year old in the middle of a snowstorm at night in the mountains. How could they possibly have any sense of direction?

They could be anywhere in the miles of dark and cold.

twenty

Jason was almost ready to end his radio contact with the sheriff when he felt Mandy straighten beneath his arm. He glanced at her, questioning her with his eyes.

"The highway."

"Hold on just a minute, Sheriff." He waited for Mandy's explanation.

"On the way back from church tonight, I pointed out the lights from the nativity to the girls as we drove by. I don't think Beth would have known how to reach here by cutting through the farm and woods like we did, but—"

"But she'd know how to follow the highway toward town," Jason interrupted, hope taking fire within him, "and look for the light on the mountainside."

Mandy nodded.

"And the highway's been closed off, so no one would have seen the girls," Tom added.

Jason explained Mandy's theory to the sheriff and signed off. "He's alerting the Highway Patrol," Jason told Mandy and Tom, "and sending some men out along the highway in a four-wheel drive and on snowmobiles."

Jason had always prided himself on being quick and decisive under fire, but the dilemma before him now made him appreciate every leader who ever made a decision involving another human life. Should the three of them stay together or split up? Should they head down the ridge to the highway and search for the girls themselves? Or stay at the nativity in case the girls showed up there?

In the end, Tom offered to stay at the nativity. Jason and Mandy started down the ridge. It was steep and rocky with few trees. "Careful. Take it slow," Jason warned Mandy. "It won't help the girls any if one of us hurts ourselves."

Yet it was frustrating to take it slow. Once Mandy lost her footing and slid full length down the slope. His heart leaped to his throat until she came to a stop thirty feet down. He wanted to shout for joy when they reached the highway where they could walk without the burden of rocks and underbrush beneath the snow.

He and Mandy continued to call as they walked along the highway toward the farm. The wind seemed to delight in tossing their voices away. They flashed their lights across the highway and along the side of the road as they walked, hoping for a glimpse of something other than trees and rocks and snow.

They rounded a bend, and the ridge became less steep, with more trees. Mandy played her light along the lower part of the ridge, where pines with sweeping, snow-covered branches stood proud.

She stopped and grabbed Jason's arm. "I thought I saw something move."

He watched her light play back over the area she'd just covered. "There. Do you see it?"

"Yes." He started toward the tree, which stood about ten feet away. Something wide and long appeared caught on a branch and swung in the wind.

Mandy plowed through the snow beside him, keeping her light trained on the branch.

As he drew closer, his certainty grew. A scarf was caught on the tree. Could it belong to Beth or Bonnie?

He tried to call out the girls' names one more time, but hope formed a lump in his throat, and he couldn't shout. He ran the last couple steps and grabbed at the scarf. It was plum-colored chenille.

His fingers clutched about the material, Jason turned to Mandy. He saw the joy in her eyes. She recognized it too.

He pulled at the scarf, but it caught. Looking closer, he saw it had been tied around the branch.

Mandy grabbed the scarf beside the knot. "Beth." The name

was barely a whisper on the wind.

Jason swallowed the lump in his throat. "Beth." It came out as soft as Mandy's, but they both kept trying. "Beth! Bonnie!"

Their voices grew louder.

"Here! We're here!"

The lower branches swung aside, dumping lumps of snow. Two red-cheeked faces peeked out.

Jason and Mandy dropped to their knees. Jason caught Beth to his chest, feeling his heart would explode through his rib cage in joy and gratitude. Beth clung to him. He saw Mandy drawing Bonnie into her embrace.

"I knew you'd come," Beth whispered between chattering teeth into his ear. "I knew you'd come."

Mandy dug the blankets and thermos from the backpacks while Jason radioed the sheriff. Shouts of rejoicing rang back over the radio waves.

A minute later the sheriff put Ellen on.

"We have a Christmas present here for you." Jason held the radio up to Beth's face.

"Merry Christmas, Mommy. Are you mad at me?"

"No, Sweetheart. Are you okay?"

"Yes."

Jason moved the radio to Bonnie. "Hi, Mommy. I want to come home. I'm c–cold."

A sob came clearly over the airwaves. "I know, Precious. Mandy and Jason will bring you home."

While Mandy and Jason wrapped the girls in blankets, Bonnie reported on their adventure. "I was c–cold. I told Beth I wanted to go home, but she said we couldn't until we found Jesus."

"I didn't think it was so far," Beth justified herself. "It didn't take very long in Tom's truck or Mommy's car."

Bonnie broke in again. "When I got really cold, I cried. Then Beth saw that tree and said let's pretend we were J. P. when he was little and crawl under it."

"The snow couldn't blow on us there," Beth explained.

"But it was still cold."

Bonnie pulled the blanket closer about her throat, shivering. "I cried lots. I was afraid nobody would find us and we'd get lost like Hansel and Gretel."

"That's why I tied my scarf on the tree, so people would see it 'cause the tree hid us."

"Very smart, Beth," Jason commended, pouring a cup of hot chocolate and handing it to her.

Beth beamed.

"I wanted to pray and ask God to bring somebody to find us and take us home so I could be warm." Bonnie glanced at Beth. "Beth didn't want to pray. She said God didn't care if anybody found us. I told her she was wrong because my Sunday school teacher says God loves us. And then I cried harder, so Beth prayed anyway. And then you came."

Two snowmobiles pulled up, followed soon after by a red Jeep. Mandy and Jason quickly bundled the girls into the warm vehicle, where Mandy helped them change from wet tights to dry jeans and socks.

There was a knock at the window and Mandy opened it.

"I'm going back with the guys on the snowmobiles to get Tom," Jason said.

Mandy frowned. "Must you? You should get out of the cold."

"I'm fine. I don't want to take a chance on the men missing Tom. I know just where to find him."

Beth pushed her chin out from the blanket. "Where's Tom?"

"At the nativity," Jason told her. "He stayed in case you and Bonnie showed up." He waved one hand. "See you all later."

"Wait." Beth struggled to sit up straighter.

Jason waited.

"My doll blanket. I think we forgot it under the tree."

"I'll get it for you." Jason started to turn away.

"No."

Jason turned back. "Don't you want it?"

"Will you take it to the baby Jesus?"

Tears heated Mandy's eyes. After all Beth had been through,

her first thought was still to protect the baby Jesus from the cold. Her determination could have cost her life and Bonnie's. One day, she'd tell her grandchildren about this adventure and laugh at what she'd perceive as her silliness. But Mandy suspected God would cherish the sweet, if misguided, desire in the little girl's heart to protect His Son.

Jason nodded solemnly. "Yes, I'll make sure your blanket covers the baby Jesus."

Beth heaved a sigh of relief. "It's a little wet. I carried it under my jacket to keep it dry, but we got cold, so when we were under the tree we put it over our legs."

"I don't think Jesus will mind that you used it first." Mandy shared a smile with Jason before rolling up the window.

The volunteers took Mandy and the girls back to the farm in the Jeep. Ellen waited at the Christmas store. Mandy watched the emotional reunion with a teary but happy heart. She called Grandma Tillie and assured her and Grandpa Seth the girls were truly home at last.

The sheriff came down to check on the girls himself before dismissing the last of his deputies and volunteers and heading home.

The girls wanted to open their Christmas presents right away—even though their pleas came between yawns—but Ellen stood firm. "It's late. You're going to take baths to warm you up and then crawl into bed. Besides, we can't open the gifts without Grandma Tillie and Grandpa Seth and Jason here. We'll have our Christmas party tomorrow morning."

Mandy was pleasantly surprised when Jason and Tom showed up half an hour after she and the girls arrived. "I thought you'd be out the rest of the night, finding your vehicles and driving them back."

"I left the Jeep, and Tom left his truck. We'll get them tomorrow. The volunteers brought us home on the snowmobiles. How are the girls doing?"

Mandy explained how the girls' hopes to celebrate Christmas yet that night had been dashed by Ellen's practical plans.

"Is Ellen holding up all right?" Tom's brown eyes looked anxious.

"She's doing fine," Mandy assured him. "She didn't even do the normal mother thing of throwing a tantrum once she realized the kids were safe. She just wants to get them warm and climb into their double bed and sleep with them."

Jason walked over to the fireplace area, picked out from the family Christmas present stack two long rectangular packages wrapped in red paper, and handed them to Mandy. "Would you ask Ellen if the girls can open these before they go to bed?"

"What did you give them?"

"You'll see."

Ellen reluctantly agreed. She'd just gotten the girls out of the tub and into clean, warm flannel nightgowns. "I don't want them getting excited over Christmas presents again and waking up. They need their sleep."

She brought the girls downstairs, where they sat on the bottom loft step to open the packages. Gasps of delight greeted the gifts.

"A puppy!" Bonnie pulled a stuffed basset hound with ears almost as long as its body from the box and hugged it to her chest. "Thank you, J. P."

Beth pulled out a matching puppy from her box. "Thanks. I'm going to call mine Old Butch."

Jason grinned. "That's a perfect name."

Bonnie frowned. "I was going to call mine Old Butch."

"Why don't you call him Little Butch?" Mandy suggested. "After all, he is a puppy."

Bonnie, with her usual compliant nature, agreed.

Ellen sent the girls off to bed. "I'll be up in a few minutes." She waited until the girls reached the top of the steps before turning to Mandy, Jason, and Tom. "There is no way I can sufficiently thank you for all you did tonight, but I promise there will always be a special place in my heart for each of you."

"We didn't do it all ourselves," Jason reminded her.

She didn't argue, just gave each of them a hug and headed

up to join her daughters.

Jason took Tom up to the farmhouse to arrange sleeping arrangements for him until morning, when the storm would hopefully abate. "Will you wait up for me?" Jason asked Mandy. "I know it's late, but I don't think I'm going to be able to sleep, and I'd like to talk to you."

So she waited for him.

There was still hot chocolate in one of the thermoses. Mandy brought two mugs down from the loft and set them on a table in the fireside area. Ellen had lit a fire in the fireplace earlier. Only glowing embers remained.

Mandy plugged in the lights of a Christmas tree near the hearth. Crystal icicles which glittered in reflected light decorated the tree. Beneath the tree, the unopened gifts were still piled, stacked in their brightly colored wrapping.

The other tree lights weren't turned on. The large, festive room felt unusually homey and comforting in the dim, mellow lighting, and the quiet was broken only by shifting embers.

She wandered idly about in the fireside sitting area, adjusting the placement of a china angel on a table or a gnome atop the mantel. A rag doll Santa Claus and his wife, dressed in red felt, sat on one corner of the hearth. Mandy knelt before them for a moment, tracing Mrs. Claus's red-stitched smile with a fingernail and running a hand over the soft white curls of the doll's hair. She pinched Santa's silky beard where it tumbled over the front of his red suit. These dolls always brought a smile to Mandy's face. Such an eternally happy-looking couple.

What did Jason want to discuss so badly he wanted to come back tonight to do so?

Mandy sat on the floor beside the dolls and stared at the embers. So much had happened inside her, in her heart and spirit, during the last few hours.

She heard the door open. The bells jangled merrily, their sound clearer and louder than usual in the night quiet.

"Mandy?"

"Over here, by the fireplace."

She could trace his movements by the sound of his footsteps on the wooden floor. In a minute he arrived at the fireside. He removed his jacket and hung it over one wing of the chair.

Mandy got up from the floor and sat down in the opposite wing chair. Only then did Jason sit down in the wing chair across from her. He rested his elbows on his knees and stared at the orange glow in the grate.

Mandy waited for him to choose his time to speak, studying his face and thinking about all the ways she loved him.

He sighed deeply. "Quite a night."

"Yes."

"Thanks for letting me come back tonight. I wanted to tell you—"

"There's something I want to say first. Please. I've been gathering my courage while I waited for you. If I don't say this right away, I might not say it all." Her heart raced as she met his gaze.

"I'm listening."

"Tonight when Ellen took the girls upstairs to bathe, I wandered through the shop. I love this store. I've loved Christmas stores from the very first moment I stepped into one."

She stopped, her gaze drifting over the shadows of trees in the dimly lit room, wondering how to put into words what was so clear in her heart. "Eight years ago when you asked me to marry you, I knew I couldn't. I knew God's place for me was in these mountains, involved in work I love."

"Mandy, I—"

She lifted a hand to silence him. If she didn't get this out, she might always regret it. "You thought I didn't love you if I wouldn't sacrifice everything for you. I did love you, but I didn't want us to end up like your parents. I only knew them through the stories you and Grandpa Seth and Grandma Tillie told me. But I know your father loved your mother so much he gave up his dreams to stay in the mountains she loved. Eventually, he grew bitter over his sacrifice. I don't know what that did to their marriage, but I know bitter hearts grow self-pitying and poison other lives."

"Our father images again."

Mandy frowned. She wanted to finish her own thoughts.

"Broken father images influencing our understanding of God," he clarified. "Remember?"

She nodded.

"I've been thinking about that a lot lately. One of the messages from my father's life was that perfect love sacrifices. And sacrifice entails giving up something we love. Suffering." His somber gaze held hers. "I was selfish to ask you to leave what you love. I don't want you to make that kind of sacrifice for me. I want you to be happy. You've been happy here, haven't you?"

"Mostly. I've loved following my dreams. But I don't need them or this place anymore to be happy." She took a deep breath and plunged on. "I don't know if there's any chance you still want me in your life, but if you do, building us is more important to me than building mountain Christmas stores."

"Mandy." With a swift, smooth movement Jason slid from the chair to the hassock in front of Mandy and gently framed her face with his hands. She saw the joy her words caused reflected in his eyes, and wonder curled through her just before his lips touched hers in a kiss so soft and so sweet it filled her with awe.

He folded his hands over hers and pressed a kiss to her fingers. "I'll never again ask you to give up your dreams for me, Mandy. But it means the world to me that you've offered."

Confusion swirled through her. When he kissed her she'd felt certain he loved her, but now. . .

"My turn to talk." He rubbed her hands gently between his. "The last couple months, seeing the way your life has played out because you stayed true to what you believe God called you to do has been a gift. You put love into your work, and that love multiplies. Following your path has allowed so many others doorways to following their own paths: Tom Berry and his mother, all the other craftspeople you've encouraged." He grinned. "The women who knitted all those mittens. You certainly gave those people a way to contribute to the world."

"You give me too much credit. People who want to contribute to the world always find places to do it." She sat up straighter, eager to share with him. "I forgot to tell you. The knitters enjoyed making the mittens so much that they've decided to work on them all year for next Christmas's mitten tree and make mufflers and hats to give away too. Isn't that wonderful?"

He laughed. "You see? You don't even realize the ways God works through your trust in the desires He puts in your heart." The laughter died away from his voice and eyes. "I realized recently that I chose the career I did because I believed my father didn't love and accept me for who I was. I fought with him until he died. Then, in a last-ditch attempt to gain his approval, I followed the example he gave me in life and sacrificed my dreams for his."

Mandy leaned forward and touched her lips to his forehead, her heart aching for the boy he'd been.

"How could I believe God wanted me to follow the dreams He put in my heart, when I couldn't believe my human father wanted me to follow those dreams? Then tonight—was it only tonight? It seems eons ago—out on the mountain in the storm, searching for the girls, everything became clear. I think my father did want me to be happy. He just couldn't see that he and I were different. He thought if I stayed in the mountains on the Christmas tree farm, I'd eventually grow as bitter as he had. He believed his only happiness lay in the financial world in a large city, so he believed that's the only place I could find happiness."

"He died young, only a few years older than you are now. He was probably just starting to figure out life himself."

"Yes." Jason splayed his fingers, touching his palms against hers. "I feel God's given me a second chance. He's given me glimpses—through you, Gramps and Gram, the girls, and

Zach—into what my life might become if I make different choices. I'm not going back to New York. I'm going to tell Gramps I want to work with him."

"Jason, that's wonderful. I mean, if it's what you want."

"It's what I want." He picked up the Mr. and Mrs. Santa Claus dolls from the hearth and sat them on his knees facing Mandy. "These remind me of the Christmas ornament we gave Gram and Gramps, the old man and woman on the bench."

Mandy smiled. "They do look similar."

"Let's get married, Mandy."

She gasped, but he didn't give her time to reply.

"Let's raise a couple great kids like Beth and Bonnie. Let's grow old together. And when we're old and gray, young couples will walk past us and say to each other, 'Will we love each other that much when we're their age?' "

Joy engulfed her heart. He remembered almost word for word what she'd said that long-ago day when they'd bought the ornament for his grandparents. She rested her palms on his cheeks and smiled into his eyes. "If those young couples are very blessed, they will love each other that much when they're old."

This time she initiated their kiss, rejoicing in the freedom to do so.

When she pulled her lips from his, Jason raised his eyebrows. "Is that a yes?"

"Oh, it's a yes, Mister. It's a yes and a promise."

He drew her into his arms, and she snuggled her head against his shoulder.

"Deep in my heart, I think I always knew you'd come back, Jason."

His arms tightened around her. "Me too." Overwhelming gratitude for her love roughened his voice. In his mind Mandy's words echoed in Beth's voice—"I knew you'd come." *Thank God, I'm finally listening.*

epilogue

Jason sat on Gram's rose-print sofa in the midst of Christmas Eve chaos. The tree with its memory-filled, humble ornaments stood as always in front of the window, pine scent filling the room. Beth and Bonnie played with new Barbie dolls, sitting on the floor surrounded by colorful, crumpled Christmas papers. A lump thickened in Jason's throat at the remembrance of Christmas Eve two years ago, when he'd wondered whether he'd ever see those two sweet girls alive again.

A slender golden retriever lay with its head touching Beth's leg. Butch seldom let the girls out of his sight. Tom had given the dog—only a wiggly puppy then—to the girls as a belated Christmas present two days after they were rescued. It took only a gentle reminder of the dog that played such an important part in saving Jason's life as a boy to convince Ellen to let the girls keep the dog.

His gaze roamed the room. Gramps and Mandy's father played chess on the small chess table that Gram had given Gramps for Christmas. Ellen and Gram sat on the floor with the girls, their own gifts stacked nearby.

There was a stir in Jason's arms, and he looked down at his son wrapped in a pale blue blanket. The bald, skinny boy, eyes closed, yawned and stretched a two-month-old arm. Then Abe nestled in again, his head resting against Jason's chest in perfect trust.

Jason's heart caught. *Don't let me ever give Abe a reason not to trust me, Lord.*

Jason realized he'd break that trust someday. It was inevitable. It was the way of humans to be imperfect. But he meant to love his children the best he knew how every day and strive to be an example of the kind of father God is.

It worked the other direction too. He'd grown to understand that in the months during Mandy's pregnancy. He had studied God's love to see how a human father should love his children. He didn't know a better gift for them.

Beth leaned against his knee and smiled down at Abe. "Good thing Bonnie and me taught you how to hold a baby, huh?"

Jason nodded. "A very good thing."

"Can I hold Abe?"

"Sure."

She climbed onto the sofa and sat close beside him. Jason laid Abe gently on her lap.

A minute later, Mandy smiled down at them. "I think Abe likes you, Beth. He certainly looks comfortable."

Beth beamed up at her.

"How's Abe's brother, Sam, doing?" Jason looked at the baby wrapped in a green blanket and held by Mandy's mother.

"Dry and happy now," the grandmother replied with a smile.

He resisted the urge to reach for his son. Mandy's parents had made the trip from Texas just to meet their new grandsons. He was glad the couple had been able to attend the twins' dedication, held during the Christmas Eve service earlier.

Bonnie pulled a fold of Sam's blanket back and peeked at Sam. "Can I hold him?"

"Wouldn't you rather open the rest of your presents?" Ellen asked.

Bonnie shook her head until her curls bounced. "No. I want to hold Sam."

Jason shared a smiling glance with Mandy as Bonnie sat down beside her sister and held out her arms. While Mandy's mother settled Sam carefully in Bonnie's lap, Mandy seated herself on Jason's lap and slipped an arm around his neck.

Jason hugged her close. The light floral scent she wore teased his senses. His heart felt warm, filled with deep thanksgiving. He loved the extended family they lived among. A slight shiver ran through him at the knowledge of how close he'd come to missing it all by stubbornly following his father's dream instead of his own. He only wished his father and mother could have met his wife and their boys.

Mandy slipped off Jason's lap and picked up four small square boxes from beneath the tree. She handed one to each of her parents and to Gram and Gramps.

The older couples "oohed" and "aahed" appreciatively over the simple crocheted ornaments that framed pictures of Abe and Sam. Gram hung her and Gramps's ornaments on the tree, near the crocheted ornament picture of Jason when he was three and those of Beth and Bonnie from two Christmases ago.

Mandy sat down on the sofa's rolled arm and leaned against Jason's shoulder. Jason glanced down at Abe, who lay in Beth's arms as though completely unaware of the excitement in the room. Sam, in Bonnie's lap, looked equally unaffected.

He never looked at those boys without joy flooding his chest.

Jason squeezed Mandy's hand and whispered, "Think Abe and Sam would like sisters for Christmas next year?"

Her eyes widened in surprise, and color flooded her cheeks. Then a smile danced in her green eyes. "It's an idea definitely worth consideration."

Jason felt delightfully tangled in her gaze, embraced in contentment and peace. He'd never suspected life could be this good, and he thanked God for the joy He'd brought to their lives.

A Letter To Our Readers

Dear Reader:

In order that we might better contribute to your reading enjoyment, we would appreciate your taking a few minutes to respond to the following questions. We welcome your comments and read each form and letter we receive. When completed, please return to the following:

Fiction Editor
Heartsong Presents
PO Box 719
Uhrichsville, Ohio 44683

1. Did you enjoy reading *For a Father's Love* by JoAnn A. Grote?
   ❑ Very much! I would like to see more books by this author!
   ❑ Moderately. I would have enjoyed it more if
   ____
   ____
   ____

2. Are you a member of **Heartsong Presents**? ❑ Yes ❑ No
   If no, where did you purchase this book? ______________
   ____

3. How would you rate, on a scale from 1 (poor) to 5 (superior), the cover design? ______________

4. On a scale from 1 (poor) to 10 (superior), please rate the following elements.

   ____ Heroine ____ Plot
   ____ Hero ____ Inspirational theme
   ____ Setting ____ Secondary characters

6. How has this book inspired your life?____________________

7. What settings would you like to see covered in future **Heartsong Presents** books? ____________________

8. What are some inspirational themes you would like to see treated in future books? ____________________

9. Would you be interested in reading other **Heartsong Presents** titles? ❑ Yes ❑ No

10. Please check your age range:

❑ Under 18	❑ 18-24
❑ 25-34	❑ 35-45
❑ 46-55	❑ Over 55

Name____________________

Occupation ____________________

Address ____________________

City__________ State______ Zip______

E-mail____________________

Presents

_HP421 *Looking for a Miracle*, W. E. Brunstetter
_HP422 *Condo Mania*, M. G. Chapman
_HP425 *Mustering Courage*, L. A. Coleman
_HP426 *To the Extreme*, T. Davis
_HP429 *Love Ahoy*, C. Coble
_HP430 *Good Things Come*, J. A. Ryan
_HP433 *A Few Flowers*, G. Sattler
_HP434 *Family Circle*, J. L. Barton
_HP437 *Northern Exposure*, J. Livingston
_HP438 *Out in the Real World*, K. Paul
_HP441 *Cassidy's Charm*, D. Mills
_HP442 *Vision of Hope*, M. H. Flinkman
_HP445 *McMillian's Matchmakers*, G. Sattler
_HP446 *Angels to Watch Over Me*, P. Griffin
_HP449 *An Ostrich a Day*, N. J. Farrier
_HP450 *Love in Pursuit*, D. Mills
_HP454 *Grace in Action*, K. Billerbeck
_HP457 *A Rose Among Thorns*, L. Bliss
_HP458 *The Candy Cane Calaboose*, J. Spaeth
_HP461 *Pride and Pumpernickel*, A. Ford
_HP462 *Secrets Within*, G. G. Martin
_HP465 *Talking for Two*, W. E. Brunstetter
_HP466 *Risa's Rainbow*, A. Boeshaar
_HP469 *Beacon of Truth*, P. Griffin
_HP470 *Carolina Pride*, T. Fowler
_HP473 *The Wedding's On*, G. Sattler
_HP474 *You Can't Buy Love*, K. Y'Barbo
_HP477 *Extreme Grace*, T. Davis
_HP478 *Plain and Fancy*, W. E. Brunstetter
_HP481 *Unexpected Delivery*, C. M. Hake
_HP482 *Hand Quilted with Love*, J. Livingston
_HP485 *Ring of Hope*, B. L. Etchison
_HP486 *The Hope Chest*, W. E. Brunstetter
_HP489 *Over Her Head*, G. G. Martin
_HP490 *A Class of Her Own*, J. Thompson
_HP493 *Her Home or Her Heart*, K. Elaine
_HP494 *Mended Wheels*, A. Bell & J. Sagal
_HP497 *Flames of Deceit*, R. Dow & A. Snaden
_HP498 *Charade*, P. Humphrey
_HP501 *The Thrill of the Hunt*, T. H. Murray
_HP502 *Whole in One*, A. Ford
_HP505 *Happily Ever After*, M. Panagiotopoulos
_HP506 *Cords of Love*, L. A. Coleman
_HP509 *His Christmas Angel*, G. Sattler
_HP510 *Past the Ps Please*, Y. Lehman
_HP513 *Licorice Kisses*, D. Mills
_HP514 *Roger's Return*, M. Davis

Great Inspirational Romance at a Great Price!

Heartsong Presents books are inspirational romances in contemporary and historical settings, designed to give you an enjoyable, spirit-lifting reading experience. You can choose wonderfully written titles from some of today's best authors like Hannah Alexander, Andrea Boeshaar, Yvonne Lehman, Tracie Peterson, and many others.

When ordering quantities less than twelve, above titles are $3.25 each.
Not all titles may be available at time of order.

SEND TO: **Heartsong Presents** Reader's Service
P.O. Box 721, Uhrichsville, Ohio 44683

Please send me the items checked above. I am enclosing **$** ______
(please add **$2.00** to cover postage per order. OH add 6.25% tax. NJ add 6%.). Send check or money order, no cash or C.O.D.s, please.

To place a credit card order, call 1-800-847-8270.

NAME ______________________________

ADDRESS ______________________________

CITY/STATE ______________________ ZIP ________

HPS 1-03